A Medieval Chri

LOVE A

Step

The STORM Series:

A Storm of Passion
A Storm of Love novella
A Storm of Pleasure
Mistress of the Storm

WARRIORS OF THE STONE CIRCLES Series:

Rising Fire
Raging Sea
Blazing Earth

A HIGHLAND FEUDING Series:

Stolen by the Highlander
The Highlander's Runaway Bride
Kidnapped by the Highland Rogue
Claiming His Highland Bride
A Healer for the Highlander
The Highlander's Inconvenient Bride – crossover with the
CLAN MACLERIE series
Her Highlander for One Night

STAND-ALONE STORIES:

The Queen's Man

The Duchess's Next Husband

The Maid of Lorne

Kidnapping the Laird

What The Duchess Wants

Upon A Misty Skye

Across A Windswept Isle

A Traitor's Heart in BRANDYWINE BRIDES

The Storyteller – A Highlanders
Through the Mists of Times Novella

An Outlaw's Honor ~ A Midsummer Knights romance

Tempted by Her Viking Enemy

The Highlander's Substitute Wife
(HIGHLAND ALLIANCES series)

A Medieval Christmas Novella

LOVE AT FIRST

Step

TERRI
BRISBIN

USA TODAY BESTSELLING AUTHOR

Love at First Step

Cover Design by Dar Albert
WickedSmartDesigns.com

Digital Formatting by Nina Pierce
ninapierce.com/book-formatting

ISBN: 978-1-949425-07-9

LUCKENBOOTH**PRESS**

Dear Reader,

I have always been fascinated by the different ways in which the holidays were celebrated throughout history, and I especially like the Scottish custom of "First Footing." It began in medieval times, and it was said that the first person through your door on the first night of the New Year (Hogmanay) determined your luck and prosperity in the coming year. It was said to have begun as far back as the Viking raids on Scotland, so a tall blond man was not the person you hoped to see that night!

The hero and heroine of my story could both use a bit of good luck in their lives. But what will happen if the man Elizabeth loves is an older, stubborn, red-haired Scottish warrior and not the dark-haired young man needed to bring her luck? Can love prevail and grant them their wishes?

I wish you and yours a happy holiday season and I hope that your first-footer brings your household much health and prosperity in the New Year!

This story is dedicated to my sons, Matthew, Andrew and Michael, who are all dark-haired heroes in the making and who give me joy in the holiday season and throughout the year. I love you all!

ONE

"Let me send her to you this night."

"Are these shorter days making you daft, man?"

Gavin MacLeod glared at his host, lifted the goblet to his mouth and swallowed deeply. The heather ale slid smoothly over his tongue and kept his other retorts quiet. He needed no help in finding a woman to bed, if 'twas his wont to do so.

He'd been visiting Orrick of Silloth at the time of the winter solstice for years and did not remember Orrick ever expressing an interest in or notice of any of the women villeins or servants before this. Of course this was his first time here since Gavin's wife's death, so mayhap Orrick felt more at ease discussing women with him now. Or was it the festive season approaching that put him more in the mind to bring up the subject?

"Look you there, Gavin. She is a whore as much as I am king of England," Orrick said, under his breath.

"Are you my procurer as well as my foster brother?"

Gavin did watch the woman now. How could he not?

Orrick's words forced his attention to her form and he noticed the attributes of most any woman were enhanced on her. Full, lush breasts, narrow waist and flaring hips, and long legs declared her attractive appearance. But instead of displaying them in an inviting way as a woman who made her living on her back usually did, this one hid them beneath a serviceable gown and veil and an almost modest demeanor.

"You are her lord, Orrick. Know you not how she makes her living?"

Orrick grunted and took a mouthful from his own goblet. For a few minutes Gavin observed this woman as she served the lower tables. She wore a ready smile on her face and spoke softly to all she served. No blatant enticement of the men was apparent in her manner and no hostility came in answer from any of the women at table. Orrick truly ran his lands and demesne differently than most English lords.

"I know how she makes a living, brother. I do not know how she came to be in that living."

Orrick's words surprised him. Orrick had a way of getting at the truth and yet this woman had kept her past a secret from him. Surprising. Intriguing. Something within him stirred for the first time in a very long time.

Curiosity.

He pushed himself into the tall-back chair on which he sat and studied her. He guessed she had about a score-and-five years. He noticed that she looked to have all of her teeth when she smiled and that her skin was clear of pox or blemish. Her back was straight as she stood; no deformity showed itself. Not the usual village harlot.

"Does it matter why she does it, Orrick? Is she causing trouble for you?"

Orrick leaned closer so his words would not be heard, most likely by Margaret, his wife, who sat on his other side. "I find an unanswered question unacceptable. Who knows what trouble she might bring if someone comes seeking her?"

Gavin felt the tug of a puppeteer's strings. He recognized his foster brother's machinations for what they were and decided that he could play at it, as well.

"Then throw her out, as is your right as lord of these lands."

The grimace and dark glare told Gavin the truth. She had stymied Orrick's quest for her story, but he would never rid his lands of even one helpless soul who lacked sanctuary. And especially not as the feast of Our Lord's Birth and the celebration of the new year approached. 'Twas ever his weakness. Gavin laughed at Orrick's plight.

"Although you are wrong in your assessment of me and in your attempts to manipulate me, I will take pity on your plight and discover the information you seek about your village whore." He nodded in the woman's direction as he spoke and nearly missed the painful look that crossed Orrick's face. Nearly.

Did Orrick have some personal interest in this woman? He thought not, but what else could explain his

3

behavior. Gavin tilted forward to check on Margaret's attention and found her in an animated conversation with the woman at her side. Now was as good a time as any to ask his question.

"Do you want her for your leman? Is that the object of all this?"

"Leman?" Orrick asked, choking on the word.

"Aye. I can find out if she is married or if there is another obstacle in your way, if 'tis your wont to claim her as your leman."

This was not such an unusual thing among nobles, but something did not feel right to him. He never would have believed that Orrick would take another to his bed while married to Margaret. It had been much too long between his visits if things between them had changed this much.

"I want no other woman but my Margaret, you thick-skulled arse," Orrick whispered furiously to him. "This is about a friend helping a friend in a task. I thought it would give you something to do while you visit with us until the new year arrives. That is all."

Relief flooded him that he would not be involved in deceiving Orrick's wife. She could be formidable in her fury and he did not want to be the one receiving such attention. And he was glad in his heart that Orrick was still as faithful to his Margaret as he had been to his wife Nessa while she lived.

"Fine, then. Send her to me and I will discover her secrets for you."

"Be discreet." Orrick whispered the warning. "The

needs of a guest cannot be ignored, but even in these long, dark days of winter Margaret cares not for whoring in her keep."

"Do not get me in trouble with your wife, Orrick. And do not get the woman—" he nodded toward their quarry "—in trouble with the lady for your curiosity."

Orrick waved off his concerns. "She will be sent to your chambers to assist you in your bath. Even Margaret will accept that. What happens from there is between you and her," Orrick said, nodding in the same direction.

Gavin sat back and took another mouthful of ale from his cup, all the time watching the graceful movements of the woman under discussion.

"Her name? You never did tell me her name, Orrick."

"Elizabeth."

Elizabeth. It was high-sounding for a whore, but it fit her graceful ways and demeanor. Her customers probably called her "Lizzie" or "Betsy," a name more suited for a woman on her back.

Elizabeth.

There! He was eyeing her again. Elizabeth watched out of the corner of her eye as Lord Orrick's friend gazed intently at her. She purposely walked to the farthest end of the rows of tables to see if he turned his look upon someone else. He did not.

Nervousness bubbled up within her as she tried to ignore what his attention meant. Although Lady

Margaret forbade her from plying her trade in the hall or keep, fulfilling the needs of an honored guest was expected. And one so high in the esteem of the lord would have every whim satisfied by anyone within the lands of Orrick.

She had done it before with others and would do it again, but she felt the uncertainty growing inside. Like some untried girl. She smiled at the miller's son as she filled his cup with ale and tried to ignore the lord's guest. Of course, with his size and his position next to Orrick at the high table it was nigh to impossible to do that. So Elizabeth decided to meet his challenge directly and raised her eyes to meet his.

His frown, even from this distance, was apparent. Had she done something to displease him already? She continued to look at him and was surprised to see the edges of his mouth begin to curl up in a smile. He was not nearly so fearsome when he smiled.

A shiver moved up her spine and she was certain that he had been discussing her with Lord Orrick. To what end? This man traveled alone, without even a squire or page or man-at-arms for his protection. The cook told her that Lord Gavin visited Lord Orrick each year at this time and usually stayed through the solstice and new year festivities before returning to his lands in Scotland.

Did he want her as a whore? Probably. She was able to recognize the intensity in his gaze as that of desire. She admitted to herself that she was not a good and practiced harlot. This was still somewhat new to her and she was

still learning the art of enticing customers and
recognizing what their looks meant. One day she would
be better at this.

One day.

She sighed and turned her attentions back to the task
she was carrying out now. The people here were kind to
her, even the men who frequented her cottage were never
rough or disrespectful to her in their actions or in the
height of their passionate attentions. For that she was
grateful. For many things she was grateful—especially
for the day she had wandered into this village and into
the demesne of Lord Orrick of Silloth. He had offered
her a place and saved her life that day. If she needed to
lie with his friends to pay back her debt to him, she would
without complaint.

Lord Orrick's friend stood and nodded at him and
took leave of Lady Margaret, as well. He was tall, taller
than the lord, who stood at least four inches past six feet.
It must be his Scots blood, for she had heard he was from
the barbaric Highlands where the men were giants and
known for their fierceness. In her thoughts she could see
him swinging a massive sword in battle against his
enemies. She shivered again, thankful that other than a
glance in her direction, she would have nothing else to
do with him.

When her jug of ale was empty, Elizabeth returned to
the pantry to fill it again. Rounding the wooden partition
that separated it from the rest of the hall, she found
herself face-to-face with the man who had just filled her

thoughts. She had to tilt her head back to meet his eyes at this closeness. His eyes, as dark a blue as she had ever seen, met hers and her mouth went dry.

She could not turn her eyes away as he smiled at her. The rugged angles of his face, the life-roughened expression in his eyes and his overwhelming size took her breath away. The jug tumbled from her grasp and landed with a thud on the floor at her feet. The steward's voice pierced her confused state as she stood staring into the Scot's icy-blue eyes.

"Lord Orrick wishes you to tend to his guest now, Elizabeth. Someone else will serve the ale."

Blinking, she looked at the steward and waited for his words to make sense. Before she could react, the man stepped back, leaned down and picked up the empty jug from the floor. Holding it out to the steward, he never moved his gaze from hers. Heat built within her and her stomach began to tighten.

"My thanks, Lord Gavin. Your bath will be ready in your chambers anon. Elizabeth? See to it now."

The orders of the steward broke her reverie. Lowering her head, she curtsied to the steward and to Lord Gavin.

"Yes, my lord."

She turned to go to the kitchens to arrange for the hot water needed for a bath. He would need the largest of their wooden tubs if there was any chance of him fitting those legs in it. Focusing her thoughts on the items needed kept her from thinking about what else this summons meant, what came after the bathing was done.

When he was clean and relaxed from the heat of the water. When he was still naked.

She shuddered, part in fear and part in anticipation of what the night would hold for her. There was something different about this man and this service. Elizabeth feared not what would happen in the joining of their bodies, but what he might do to the heart she kept hidden so well. And she did not know why he felt like such a threat to her.

Two

She tested the steaming water with her elbow and nodded, pleased that it was hot enough but not too. Looking over the small bottles and jars on the tray, she chose several and added an amount of each to the water. Fresh and soothing scents filled the chamber as the oils mixed with the steaming water. Stirring them with her hand, she nodded again. The bath was ready, but where was Lord Gavin?

As if his name in her thoughts had conjured him from nothing, the door opened and he stood just within the frame. Silhouetted by the torches in the corridor, she could see nothing but the outline of his form.

"'Tis ready, my lord." She walked to the door as he stepped into the room. Trying to keep in as much heat as possible, she closed the door behind him. Beads of sweat, from both her exertions and from the heat, trickled down her neck and back. Using the back of her hand, she wiped it from her brow.

The man stood before the large tub and just stared at it. Was there a problem? What did he need?

"My lord?" she asked. "Is something wrong?"

"Did you pick out the scent yourself?"

"Aye, my lord. The oils are from Lady Margaret and will soothe the roughness and dryness of your skin. If they are not pleasing to you, I could change them."

It would take four servants each carrying two large buckets of heated water to refill the tub, but it could be, would be, done if he so wished.

"I should have waited for you before adding them, my lord. I beg your pardon." She leaned her head down respectfully, awaiting his decision. In truth, she chose the scented oils that reminded her of the coming festivities— pine, holly berry, and Lady Margaret's precious balsam.

"I asked because 'twas an appealing combination, not because it displeased me."

Turning away, she busied herself organizing what she would need for his bath. Cloths, jars of soap, extra buckets of water, drying linens. She laid them out near the tub so she could reach them easily as she needed them. All in an effort to avoid watching him undress. When she could wait no longer, she looked across the room to where he remained fully dressed and watching her every move.

"The water is cooling, my lord," She said as she held out her hand over the bath. "Do you need help with your...?" She did not finish the words, but simply pointed to him.

"I am not such a bairn that I need help getting undressed," he answered in a voice so deep and smooth that it reminded her of warm honey, fresh from the hive on a summer's day.

"No, my lord. I did not mean that."

He seemed bothered by something. Was she not brazen enough toward him? Was he waiting for her to take charge of this? After all, everyone knew that a male guest asking for "a bath" was simply another way to speak of their desire to tup. Elizabeth stepped closer and reached for the ties on his tunic.

"Nay, lass," he said, stepping back. "I can take off my own clothing."

His words were not harsh, but she felt the rebuke. Mayhap she had misread the situation? She would not overstep her place again with him. Turning her back to him, she walked to the side of the tub and waited there. Busying herself by checking the water, she did not watch his movements. Elizabeth could see him out of the corner of her eye and when he turned his back to her, she took advantage of the chance to take a closer look at him.

He was of the same age as Orrick, having just over two score of years, and his experience as a warrior showed on his body. The scars of old wounds covered parts of his back and even one thigh, but they did not detract from his physical beauty. His long, dark red hair, unmarked by gray, fell below his shoulders. Wide, brawny shoulders they were, as was his back. A narrow waist and hips led to strong, muscular legs. The perfect male body. She sighed, imagining what the front of him would look like. So deep in her thoughts was she that she did not notice him turn at the sound she made.

Aye, he was impressive. And he was watching her as she watched him! Now, he stood before her, naked as the day his mother birthed him.

Blinking quickly, Elizabeth turned her face to the tub and cleared her throat. How incredibly stupid to be attracted to such a man! He would bathe, take his pleasure on her and be gone from her life by the morn. Apparently, the hard lessons of the past year of her life were not yet learned well enough.

"Watch your step, my lord. The oils make the tub a bit slippery when you step into it." She hoped that concentrating on the bath would lessen the tension she felt between them.

Without a word, Lord Gavin walked to the tub, stepped into the heated water, turned around and sat down. As she had suspected, his long legs did not fit so he drew them up, his knees now exposed above the tub's rim.

Without delay, she lifted one of the jars, scooped out a generous handful of the soft soap and shared it between her hands. Pushing his hair off his back with her hand, she spread the soap over his shoulders, down his back and around again. Taking a cloth, she dipped it into the water and lathered the soap until the thick foam covered his back.

Elizabeth moved to the side and lifted his arm to

continue the washing. She noticed his eyes were closed, but she doubted that he was asleep. He allowed, even aided, her work as she moved around him, washing his limbs. He lifted one leg out of the tub and then the other as she spread the soap over him. It was as she began to scrub his chest and stomach that he stopped her with his larger hand over hers.

"I can do the rest, lass. If you would move the bucket of rinse water for me and leave it where I can reach it, you may go."

"My lord?" Elizabeth did not understand his dismissal. "Have I done something to displease you?"

"Nay, lass. The bath has been pleasant and well-done. 'Tis all I need from you."

Elizabeth nodded, still surprised that he did not want bed-play as other men would. She knew she was not the best-looking of women, but she had washed her face and tidied herself before coming here tonight. Was there something wrong with her? Mayhap he did not frequent whores?

She walked to the hearth in the chamber and moved one of the three buckets of clean water closer to the tub. The lord had dipped his head into the tub and was scrubbing his scalp as she moved the cloths and drying linens to where he could reach, always watching his movements in the tub. She also moved an empty bucket for rinsing his head nearer to him.

"Lass? It looks like I do need your help. Would you pour that water over my head?"

A nervous tension grew within her. Although his manner was straightforward, she felt as though he was toying with her. But, why?

"Aye, my lord," she answered as she lifted the bucket as high as she could.

Lord Gavin leaned his head back over the side of the tub so that the water would flow into the empty bucket. Elizabeth poured the warm, clean water over him and he rubbed to remove the soap from his hair. As she put down the bucket, he twisted the length of his hair, releasing most of the water it held.

Then he stood up.

She was trapped between the tub and the bed and had nowhere to look or move as he stretched to his full height and stepped out of the tub. Beads of water sluiced down his body, over every muscle from neck to chest to thighs and down. She was unable to look away as he used one of the drying cloths to press more water from his hair and then he wiped his body once. Their eyes met and Elizabeth found that her breath and voice had left her.

"What other tasks do you have this night, lass?"

His voice made her toes curl and a pool of heat formed in her belly. This was startling. She had been tupped by many men since her arrival here and this mix of fear and anticipation surprised her. Why did he not simply take his pleasure and be done?

"None, my lord, save you. Lord Orrick said I should tend to you only." How she had forced the words out, she knew not.

"The water is still warm and nigh to clean. Use it if you would like," he said, pointing to the tub, completely comfortable in his nakedness.

"A bath? Me?" The opportunity for a bath in a tub of warm water did not come often to her, and especially not in the dead of winter. Being second in would also be a treat. But she would need to undress here to take it.

He laughed and the sound of it echoed through the chamber. Lord Gavin was a handsome man and when he smiled, an attractive set of dimples formed in his rugged cheeks giving him a much younger appearance. She watched as he nodded at her.

"Aye, lass. For you, if you be wanting to enjoy it."

She worried her bottom lip as she thought on his offer. She was about to refuse when he laughed again.

"I am to bed now, lass. If you would put out the candles when you leave?"

Elizabeth nodded her head, still in disbelief, as he did just as he said. He tossed the cloths in a pile near the hearth and, after pulling several blankets off the rope-strung bed, he climbed in and made himself comfortable. He rearranged the pillows and then turned on his side facing away from her. Deciding that to pass up this chance was foolish, Elizabeth moved quietly to the side of the tub.

"May I, my lord? Truly?" Part of her wanted to tear off her soiled garments and jump in. Another part urged caution with this man who was unknown to her.

"'Twould be folly to waste good bathwater. 'Tis yours to use," he answered without moving.

"My thanks to you," she whispered as she tugged at the laces on her gown. If she moved quickly, she could wash, dry herself and be dressed in a few minutes. If she was quiet, he would fall to sleep and never even know she was still here.

She loosened her gown and pulled it over her head. Then her shift, stockings and shoes followed, and she stepped into the tub and sat as soundlessly as she could. She could not, however, stop the sigh of pleasure that escaped as the heat soothed her tired body. The tub in which he barely fit gave her nearly enough room to lie back.

After unraveling her braided hair and dipping beneath the water, she lathered and washed and rinsed as quickly and silently as she could. Only a few minutes had passed when she twisted the length of her hair to squeeze out the water and prepared to stand. Elizabeth did not know what made her look up, but there he stood with a bucket of the clean water held up to rinse her free of the soap and dirt from the now twice-used bathwater.

And he was still naked.

She swallowed several times trying to think of what to say and trying not to look at his body. 'Twas a difficult task since he was so close and so…large.

She was being an empty-headed ninny. She was a whore and had been for several months now. Why did this one man cause such nervousness within her? They would tussle. They would tup. She would leave. Nothing different from the other men who had used her body before him.

With a renewed sense of her place in this, she stood and waited for him to pour the water over her. She did have to struggle with herself not to raise her arms to cover herself from his sight. Instead, she concentrated on the warmth of the water as it flowed over her head and down the rest of her. She had not been this clean…in months. When she wiped her eyes clear, she saw Lord Gavin standing with his hand outstretched to her, to help her step from the tub.

Elizabeth accepted it and found herself wrapped in a drying cloth and standing before the hearth, absorbing its heat. 'Twas pure luxury, she knew, but if this was the way he would pay her, she was tired and dirty enough to accept it. Of course, as Lord Orrick's guest, there was no fee to be paid. Without a word, he walked back to the bed and climbed in it.

"My lord," she said, turning to him. "My thanks for sharing your bath. Should I call the servants to remove the tub now?"

"Nay, lass. Leave it until morn."

She hesitated, not sure of what to do or where to go. He watched her every move. Finally she decided not to delay his pleasure any longer. This sense of unbalance in her that his nearness and his looks and his voice caused within her had to end. She unwrapped the cloths from around her and walked to the bed, not hiding from him.

A woman's naked flesh seemed to get most men ready for tupping and she expected that he would grab her and take her now.

He did nothing but look at her. Slowly his gaze moved up and down over her, making her breasts tighten and sending waves of heat through her belly. Elizabeth did not recognize these feelings and was not certain if she wanted them to stay or go. Lord Gavin turned from her for a moment and she realized he was holding the covers out for her to enter the bed, but he offered her the side of the bed away from the door of the chambers. After a momentary hesitation, she walked around and climbed in next to him.

Elizabeth lay next to him, enjoying the comfort of the overstuffed mattress and the smell of the clean sheets on it. The thin pallet on which she slept here and the one in her cottage offered nothing close to the feeling of floating that this one did. She sighed and allowed herself a moment before turning her attentions to the naked man beside her.

He smiled when she looked at him. Were her small comforts humorous to him? Most likely since he was accustomed to such. She had been, as well… before. His expression turned serious and she expected that 'twas time to begin.

"Sleep well, lass."

Lord Gavin shifted on the mattress and arranged the bed-covers several times before seeming to find a comfortable position. He was going to sleep. Sleep?

"My lord? Is there something else?"

"Nay, lass. I asked for a bath and I had it. 'Tis all I wanted this night."

"But my lord…" She began to push the blankets off her. "I should go."

"And rest on a dusty pallet in the hall? Now that you are clean, why not rest here this night?" His hand on hers stayed her leaving.

His voice held compassion and caring in its deep, velvety tones and Elizabeth fought the tears that burned in her throat. No one, not even Lord Orrick, had treated her with this much concern in years and years and she felt herself weakening in the face of it. Did he know what he did to her? Did he know that he could destroy her with such consideration?

"If you wish, my lord." She would rest the blame on him.

"I wish it, lass." His thick burr curled around his words and she felt his heated breath next to her ear.

So be it then. Elizabeth sank into the mattress and the heat of his grasp on her hand spread through the rest of her. Tired from hours of serving meals and cleaning in the kitchens, she could feel sleep taking its hold of her.

"My name is Elizabeth," she whispered, for no reason she could think of.

"Sleep well, Elizabeth."

"Any success in our quest?"

Gavin glared at Orrick as he seated himself next to his host at the table in order to break his fast. Lady Margaret was nowhere to be seen this morn. A serving girl placed a tankard in front of him before he could ask for it.

"*Our* quest? I did not know you were working on this with me." He drank deeply of the ale.

"Do not quibble with me, Gavin. Did you find the answers I seek or not?"

Orrick was testy this morn. Good. Served him right to feel the frustration that he himself felt. Well, he was certain 'twas not the exact same frustration. He delayed answering by drinking again and then calling for food and waiting for its arrival.

The mealy porridge served here did not compare with the hearty one served at his keep, but 'twould have to do. The food here would not vary much in substance or amount until the feasting days of the anniversary of Our Lord's Birth and the twelve nights after it. For now, the serving girl familiar with his ways placed a bowl of porridge, a jar of honey and a jug of cream before him. The steward brought out a small skin of *uisge beatha,* whisky, to him and he mixed it into the steaming porridge. Soon it smelled much more appetizing than the original did. He ignored Orrick's glare and spooned several mouthfuls in before stopping.

"No answers yet."

"She spent the night in your chambers, Gavin. What did you do?"

"The usual things a man does with a woman in the night." He could not help himself. Orrick was such a pleasure to goad into a reaction and this one was not long in coming.

"Blast you," he whispered harshly. "Tell me what you learned."

Gavin smiled at Orrick's displeasure and could not resist drawing this out a bit more. "We bathed and we slept."

"Expect a challenge as soon as the weather clears, friend."

"Orrick, if your words did not say otherwise, I would swear I hear jealousy in your voice."

Orrick exhaled loudly and sat back in his chair. "Not jealousy, Gavin. Concern at a wrong done to an innocent."

Orrick had always been too soft when it came to his people. He coddled them and treated them as though they were much more than simply his property. Gavin had never quite understood it until Orrick had explained it as his application of the Scottish clan system on his English estate. Clan was about more than property and lands, it was about family and belonging. Orrick gave his villeins a sense of belonging, even though his authority was clear and never challenged.

"We bathed and slept and no more than that. Truly."

"Do not use her, Gavin. I did not ask you for help to play her falsely."

"She has proclaimed herself a whore. If she is not one, then, as her lord and master, forbid her to play that role."

"I tried that. It did not work." Orrick's tone was sullen.

"What did she do?" Gavin recognized the same stubborn streak in Elizabeth that had gotten him in trouble many, many times.

"She refused food. She told me quite boldly that she would earn her way and not be beholden to anyone."

"Did you not offer her work in your hall? Or in your laundry? Or your kitchens?" Gavin thought that those places would be a good place if a woman could work but had no skills.

"She asked if we had a harlot in the village and when I said not, she said that was how she earned her living in the past."

"So, where is the problem, Orrick? I think you make too much of this." The tightening in his gut told Gavin that there was something more here. How did you help someone who did not want help?

"Discover her secrets so I can let this go."

"I told you I would. You act like an old woman instead of the Orrick I knew."

His friend said nothing but clapped him on the back and left him to his food. Gavin turned back to his still-hot porridge and contemplated his methods.

He had had her off balance—she fully expected to be bedded when he called for a bath. And when she bent over him, spreading the soap on his flesh with a thorough but soft touch, his body had reacted as it should. 'Twould be no hardship to lay her on the bed and take her. And take her again.

'Twas more important to his task to build her trust and so he'd ignored his body's demands and forced himself to sleep next to her.

Although he did not admit it to Orrick, he was certain that she had not been raised a whore. There was a moment or two during the night when a look of fear or uncertainty entered her eyes and when she seemed to be convincing herself of what she needed to do. And it did not come easily to her.

So, why then did she force herself to do this when Orrick had offered her a different way? What loss had she suffered that made her seek her own way in this world, especially since the world was an unkind place for most everyone?

Gavin looked out over the hall to see if she was serving the tables. He'd awakened to find her still deeply asleep and he had hesitated to wake her. 'Twas obvious she had enjoyed the bath. The sound of her sigh as she slipped beneath the water had weakened his resolve not to touch her and he found the excuse he needed when he spied the bucket of rinse water. And the enjoyment in her eyes as he wrapped her in the drying cloth made his mouth water.

She was no whore, but she was an enticing woman who had reawakened desires he had ignored for a very long time. That alone made her a danger to his well-established life.

So tonight, he would summon her again and build more trust before asking his questions. He almost felt guilty over how easy this would be….

Almost.

THREE

His chamber was ready. Servants had brought him a selection of foods, some hot, some cold, some plain and some more elaborate. They all had one thing in common—they were temptations for his use. In the middle of winter, food tended to become plain and monotonous. With the lord's permission and the cook's help, Gavin had planned a feast for Elizabeth. When all was ready, he sent a servant to summon her. Her knock came just a few minutes later.

"You called for me, my lord?"

Her voice was quiet and she stood just outside the door. He waved her in and walked over to close the door behind her. Her eyes resembled a deer surrounded in the forest by hunters with no escape route left to it. She surveyed the room, from corner to corner, past the bed and back to him.

"I asked for a meal and they sent up enough to feed several people. I know you served the meal in the hall and did not eat yet, so I thought you might join me."

"I could not, my lord," she said with a curtsy. "I take my meals in the kitchen after my duties are done." He could see she was gauging her distance to the door and his position there.

"Your duties are done for tonight, Elizabeth. Orrick said I could have you now."

He purposely chose the words to make her think his intent was physical. And from the way her breathing changed and her eyes widened, he had been successful. His own erection spoke of his success, too.

She lowered her head and curtsied once more. "As you wish, my lord."

"I am not your lord. Call me Gavin."

She looked up, startled by his familiarity and shook her head. "I could not do that, my lord."

"In Scotland, we do not fall back on such formality as you do here. My given name is what my retainers, my family and even my enemies call me. Surely, you are brave enough to use it."

Elizabeth looked torn over what to do, but then she nodded her answer. "I cannot join you for this meal. 'Twould be unseemly."

"Ah, you cannot join me to eat, but you could share my bed if 'twas my wish? Is that what you are telling me?"

She did not answer him, and he wondered if she was thinking on the absurdity of it. Well, there was more than one way to get closer to her.

"'Tis a fine idea, lass. Get on the bed, then."

He pointed to the bed and watched as, with an air of resignation, she crossed the room to it. As she had done last night, she climbed on it from the side farthest from the door and waited. When he did not move, she began to loosen the ties on her gown.

"Nay, not yet," he said. "You may not be hungry, but I am."

Gavin saw the surprised look on her face but ignored it to sit by the table. He thought about facing away from her for a moment, however he decided to face the hearth so he could still watch her expressions. Her reactions began as soon as he tore the leg off a capon and bit into it. The juicy meat was hot and seasoned, and he ate it with gusto.

Her mouth tightened and a frown crossed her brow, but she said not a word. Gavin increased the pressure on her by choosing another chunk of meat from the platter before him and putting it in his mouth. Chewing for a moment, he washed it down with a mouthful of Margaret's special ale.

The silence was broken by the noisy rumbling of a stomach—and it wasn't his. His amused gaze met her embarrassed one and he fought to keep the threatening smile from his face. He lost the battle and broke out laughing.

"I told you to eat," he said, holding out a chunk of steaming bread. "There is plenty for both of us."

He watched the battle raging within her. Her hunger was obvious from the rumblings of her belly; the ravenous light in her eyes intensified as she followed his every move. When it looked as though she would continue to resist his efforts, he chose another piece of roasted beef and took it to her. Sitting down beside her on the rope-strung mattress, he held it out in front of her mouth, urging without words that she take it from his fingers.

Gavin knew the moment he had won this battle, for she tilted her head slightly and lifted her mouth to his hand. In spite of knowing it was only a way for him to gain control, he discovered that he was not immune to her after all. The touch of her lips on his fingers as she finally accepted the food jolted him from head to toe, mostly in between. He could not move his hand away even after she took the meat and began chewing it.

Shaking himself free of her spell, he returned to the table and brought his goblet back to her. As she finished chewing, he lifted it to her lips and tilted it for her to drink. In his inexcusable haste, he let some of the ale spill over. He watched as it trickled down from her mouth, onto her neck and then under the thin layer of the chemise under her gown. His mouth hungered to follow it, so he did.

He nipped and licked the path of the spill, his tongue feeling the pounding of her pulse under the delicate skin of her neck, the tense panting that began as he moved lower and the heat of her skin as he tasted his way down toward her breasts. He grew hard and he shifted to accommodate himself in his breeches. But when she drew back, he accepted the message and moved away.

She was afraid of him.

Did she fear him as a man or think him a Scots barbarian as so many in England did? Or was it something else? Did she fear that he would discover her secrets, her weaknesses, and use them against her? Gavin slid from the bed and went to the table, sitting and eating more from the platters of food before him. He would bide his time.

Mayhap not.

He took a few more bites of meat and mouthfuls of ale before speaking again. Elizabeth sat as still as stone on the bed where he'd left her. Only her eyes moved, fastened onto his every gesture. She was like no whore he'd ever met.

"Are you afeard of me, lass?"

The emotions flitted across her face—a fierce frown on her brow, a tightening of those lips he wanted to claim. Even her breathing had not slowed. He saw the struggle within her as she attempted to answer his question and the challenge within it.

"I know many Sassenachs that are afraid of us. Scots warriors are known for our ferocity and—"

Her laughter surprised and interrupted him. This was an unexpected turn.

"You must not know the true nature of the Scots if you can laugh at my words."

The sound of it echoed through the chamber and he wanted to drink it from her lips. Her face changed as she laughed and all the tension was released. She looked years younger when a smile graced her. How many years did she have?

"My grandmam told me the true nature of Scottish men, my lord. They like their whisky strong, their nights of drinking it long, and their women to ignore it." Elizabeth smiled again, but the way her eyes looked off in the distance told him she was remembering something…someone from her past. "Change the drink and that describes most men of any origin."

Something within him was insulted at first, but he realized that her lot in life had shown her only that part of men. The laughter burst out from him and he did not try to restrain it. She had spirit when she wasn't trying to be so plain. Gavin looked at her once more and realized this truth—she was a beautiful woman hiding it in a work gown and kerchief.

"Is that all you know of men?" He probed for more than the knowledge he'd received already.

Elizabeth sat up straighter on the bed and rearranged her gown so she could sit cross-legged. He watched her struggle with an answer.

"I know much of men, my lord. Their actions, their desires." Her eyes flashed at the mention of desires, yet her look was not one of wanting but of loathing.

"And what of women's desires? What know you of them?"

Her chin lifted and regret and loss entered her expressive eyes. Did she know how much she gave away with simply a glance? "Women have no desires, my lord. At least not for more than a safe place to live."

Gavin was saddened by her words—they struck deeply within him, for in his experience women lived life to the fullest. He knew that his late wife met him match for match in her appetites for living and loving. How empty had Elizabeth's existence been that she believed this and would rather be a whore to men's desires than have her own? He watched her gather her control around herself and he knew that another direct question would be deflected. What had she told him? Her grandmam knew the Scots?

"Was your grandmam Scottish herself?"

"Aye, my lord. But from the Borders, not the Highlands like you."

"Did you live with her? Or she with you?" he probed, suspecting that her relative was a safe subject. Gavin chose to turn his attentions back to his food as though this were unimportant chatter.

"I was only a girl when she died, my lord," Elizabeth said. A soft smile crossed her face. "I remember many of her sayings."

"All about men?" He lifted a chunk of bread and tore off a piece with his teeth,

"Nay, she had wisdom about many things. Mostly I remember her songs."

"Come, lass. Share the food with me." He tried once more to get her to the table.

Her stomach betrayed her hunger again and Elizabeth decided that eating with him would be the least of the dangers he offered. She tugged on the laces of her chemise and slid off the bed, accepting his invitation. She had had no chance to eat an evening meal yet and, as he'd said, there was more than enough for both of them. She sat on a stool on the opposite side of the table from him and waited.

"Dinna be shy," he said with a brogue she had noticed only once before. He pushed a few of the platters closer to her and even poured her a mug of ale.

Making up her mind to enjoy the wondrous meal before her, she chose a variety of the dishes and went about eating them. Licking her lips, she marveled at the assortment, especially in the middle of winter when the food in the hall did not include such choices.

"You must have bribed the cook to get such a feast," she said.

"I did," he answered with no hint of guile or guilt.

"Why? Surely the meal in the hall was filling enough?" The gravy of a meat pasty leaked down her chin and when she looked for a napkin to catch it, she found his beneath her chin. With his hand wiping her lips. She must learn to let go of the past and simply use her sleeve. Elizabeth waited on his answer and was not certain he would give one. His eyes turned serious and then heated, and she began to fear his response.

"For you, lass. To entice you into my chambers."

With a sense of resolution, she understood this now.

He was paying for her services. There was nothing else to it. Somehow it was easier now that she knew, and she began the process within her mind and soul to try to detach herself from the act that would happen soon.

"I will lie with you if you desire it, my lord," she said. Pointing to the table covered with food, she continued, "You do not need to go to this extent and effort. As my lord Orrick's guest, I could not accept payment from you anyway."

He surprised her then, pounding his fists on the table, making his goblet and her mug shake and wobble. His face flushed red and she saw his expression turn hard. How had she insulted him? What could she do to assuage his anger?

"I do desire it and I have been foolish to delay my pleasure. 'Tis past time to bed you."

His words were exactly the opposite of ones he'd spoken last night. 'Twas only a matter of time with men before taking their pleasure overcame any hesitation or other distractions. He was proving to be the same as the others who had come before him and would come after in her bed. Elizabeth could understand that, but she could not explain the deep sense of sadness within her at the realization.

He stood and came around the table toward her. As she rose to meet him, she worked to find the calm place inside her where she could hide until this was over. His kiss, when it came, was not the overpowering one she expected, but a soft touch on her lips. It was devastating.

He wrapped his arms around her and half-walked, half-carried her to the bed, and she found herself sinking into the softness of the mattress and covered with the hard planes of his body. His lips never lifted from her and the kiss deepened until she felt the heat of him pouring into her. He tasted and savored and touched. His mouth devoured hers and his hands began to explore her body.

As she had before, she pulled back and relaxed her body, letting him have his way. She was hardly aware of it when he lifted her skirts and loosened her chemise to gain access to her flesh. She focused on the roughness of the skin of his fingers and not on where they touched. She closed her eyes and let her thighs fall open, allowing him to enter her.

Elizabeth's thoughts wandered as she heard his moans and as he moved within her. 'Twould not be long now for he was nearing his climax. Soon, it would be over and she would clean herself of any signs of this joining and find her pallet for the night. His insistent voice broke into her reverie.

"Elizabeth? Look at me, lass." His voice was thick with his passion as she opened her eyes. She struggled to gather her thoughts and look at his face above hers. She realized he was still hard within her.

"My lord?" she asked, wondering why he called her name.

A stricken expression filled his face as she felt his seed spilling within her. She waited for him to finish and to withdraw, but he held himself still and simply stared at her as though waiting for something from her.

"My lord?" she asked again. "What have I done wrong?"

This attention unnerved her and she felt exposed before him. Usually, the man saw to his pleasure, finished and left before she had to do anything. This was so different.

Finally he lifted himself off her and stood next to the bed, pulling his breeches back around his waist and shoving his tunic over them. Elizabeth pushed her own skirts down over her legs and slid back against the headboard of the bed. Now he would not meet her gaze. He brushed his hair from his eyes and ran his hand through it, confusion clear on his face and in the frown on his brow. He looked around the room as though he had lost something. Then he looked directly at her and the pain in his eyes pierced her.

"Do not leave," he ordered even as he grabbed a long cloak from a peg on the wall near the door. His harshness was unlike anything else that had been spoken by him before and it scared her. Then he tugged open the door and, as it slammed behind him, he was gone.

For the first time since the early days of making her own way in the world, Elizabeth felt used… soiled. The calm acceptance of her situation that she had struggled to attain shattered around her and she did not know how to piece it back together.

His head pounded as he climbed the stairs that led to the roof of the keep. Gavin knew only that he needed to get away from the scene of his crime and consider how to go on from here. All his plans to entice and seduce had turned on him and in an instant when she offered herself so calmly to him, all he could think of was claiming her and shattering that resolved expression from her eyes. He was a damned fool.

He reached the fourth floor and pushed through the door leading into the frigid wind that buffeted the top of Silloth Keep. The storm that had raged for days around them, forcing them to live inside, now began to abate. Still, the cloak he'd thrown around his shoulders was pulled and twisted as he moved from the doorway. The lone guard assigned to this location nodded at him from the small stone enclosure and he walked on into the dark and cold.

Making his way to the edge of the wall, Gavin peered into the darkness and tried to understand what had just happened. Never, never in his memory had he lost control of himself as he had with Elizabeth. Something in her air of resignation challenged him and for a moment he was determined to make it different for her. He would not be like the others who lay with her and took of her. He would not pay for her favors. He would make her want him and want to…

The stupidity of his thoughts shocked him. She had ceased to be a person to him and had become only a means to an end. Orrick's quest had become his own and he used any means, even her, to succeed in it. And he had become just one more man in her bed.

He pushed his hair back from his face and gathered it in a leather thong he kept in his cloak. He walked a few paces and rubbed his eyes, trying to see into the darkness around him. The winds swirled and he let them beat against him. It was nothing compared to the chaos of feelings within him.

He closed his eyes and saw in his thoughts the moment he realized what he was doing. They were already on the bed and he had filled her to her core. Ignoring the reality of her reaction, he had plunged in and was nearing his peak when he looked at her, really looked at her for the first time. She lay beneath him, unmoving, taking everything he gave and never responding. Oh, her woman's flesh was soft and wet as he moved within her, but she was not feeling him. She was not feeling anything at all. He thought her unconscious when she did not open her eyes at her name.

But it was far worse when she did look at him with cold, unseeing eyes. Her vacant stare forced him to think and to realize what he was doing. He was taking her. He was with a woman who was not even aware of what was happening between them. A woman who lay as one dead beneath him.

The shudder that tore through him had nothing to do with the bitter cold around him. It was about the coldness within him for his mindless tupping of a woman who had no choice in it. That was something that he had never done—not even from his earliest experiences with lust and the sins of the flesh.

Under his breath, he cursed his lapse in control and judgment, and wondered how it had happened at all and how he could correct this. The crunching steps signaling the approach of the guard drew his attention.

"My lord, Lady Margaret awaits you within and requests that you join her."

With a nod, he followed the man back across the roof to the doorway and pulled the door open. Orrick's wife stood just inside and stepped aside to allow him to enter. She said nothing but turned down the hallway and made her way to a small alcove. He pulled off his wet cloak and threw it over his shoulder.

"There is some trouble, my lord?" Margaret's words carried the soft accent of her youth.

"None that I know of, lady."

Her focus sharpened and she tilted her head, examining him closely. "My lord husband told me of your special arrangements for the evening and of the task he set for you regarding the young wh… woman Elizabeth. Now, you slam out of your chambers and stalk to the roof. Something is not right?"

Damn! Orrick should have kept this between them. Women had a strange way of looking at some things and the lady of the keep was not one to be told of arrangements between men.

"Worry not, my lady. All is well." He was not about to explain what had happened in his chambers. He shifted on his feet and prepared to end the conversation when her words shocked him.

"Will she need the services of our healer, my lord?"

Margaret thought he had hurt Elizabeth. The insult of it lashed him to his soul. He had not treated her well, but she had not been harmed. He had never taken a woman in anger. Never.

"Margaret! You know me better than that. How can you ask such a thing?" But a niggling of guilt slid through him. Her words confirmed it.

"My lord, I have heard how well you treated your wife, but whores are a different matter, are they not?"

He met her steely regard and knew she spoke of many things in her own past. He knew the story of how Margaret moved from being the king's whore to being Orrick's wife. This was far too personal to continue.

"I assure you that Elizabeth is well, lady. And now that I am done my walk, I will seek my chambers for the night." He nodded a bow to her and began to turn when he realized that he had a question for her. "Do you worry about Orrick's attention to her?"

Margaret smiled and lowered her gaze for a moment. "You mean that he seeks her company or favors?" He nodded. "Nay, my lord. You see I know that, by his very nature, Orrick draws strays and wounded creatures to him. He gives them sanctuary while they mend and then they are loyal to him forever."

"You think that Elizabeth is one of these strays?"

"Just so, my lord. As are we all."

Then, with a nod of her own, Lady Margaret moved past him and left him standing in the corridor. Gavin heard her words and realized the truth in them, but his thoughts turned to the woman he'd left behind in his room.

FOUR

The door opened quietly and she would have missed it had she not been watching for it. He entered like someone not sure of what he would find inside. And since she was not certain of how he would react, she knew the feeling well. He looked around the room until he found her, sitting in the far corner, away from the food and the bed—the two temptations of the evening. Well, two of three if the truth be told, for he was as tempting to her as the others had been.

"Lass," he said as he pulled the chair away from the table and turned it. Straddling it backward, he faced her. "Did I hurt you?"

She sat up straighter on the stool and gathered the blanket around her shoulders. His words were soft and she could feel his concern for her well-being in them. Why did he do this to her? What was it about him that was so different from the others? And why did part of her yearn for the difference he offered?

"I am well, my lord. I waited as you ordered."

Elizabeth watched him as he searched for words. Something had not gone correctly in their joining and he struggled with it, she could see. Unfortunately, she knew not what it was and so could offer him no help.

"I lied to you, Elizabeth." He shifted on his chair and looked away from her. Glancing at the table still laden with uneaten foods, he continued, "I did arrange this to entice you here, but I had no intention of... of bedding you this night."

She did not know what to make of his words. "My lord, I confess that I am confused. You know I am a whore and you invited me to your chambers. For what other purpose than your desire to have a woman would you ask me here?"

"For your company. To share a meal and some conversation."

No man had wanted her company since her husband in the early years of their marriage when he still kept up the pretense of interest. After that, he still desired her body, but only in an attempt to gain an heir. Gavin MacLeod made no sense. Then, she thought she understood what had happened.

"You are married, my lord?"

"Married?" He looked startled at her question.

"Aye, married and feeling some sense of guilt for lying with me? Did you make some vow to your wife that you believe broken by what we did?"

That stricken look was back in his eyes again and Elizabeth knew she had the right of it. That he was so upset at breaking a vow to his wife touched her somehow. 'Twas a good thing to know that some men actually believed in keeping their marriage vows and that he considered his lying with her, a whore, a violation of that vow. Most men did not.

"My wife is dead these last three years, lass. And lest you think differently, I never broke my promise of fidelity to her during our twenty years of marriage."

"I meant no insult to your honor or to her memory, my lord. 'Tis just that most men believe that lying with a whore does not mean anything to any vow they've taken."

His brow furrowed with a deep frown and she wondered what was wrong. He was a curious man, unlike any other she'd known. His explanation proved her right in that assessment.

"Hold now, lass. Let me begin again. When Orrick pointed you out in the hall—" He paused and cursed under his breath. "When you helped me with my bath last evening, you seemed tired. I thought mayhap you would enjoy a few hours of leisure and a good meal. Since I wanted some simple companionship, this meal seemed like the way to accomplish something for both of us."

He stood then and moved his chair back near the table. Then he poked around the dishes there until he found something he was looking for and turned to her.

"There is still the cook's wondrous spiced cake to eat. From past years, I know we'll not see the likes of it again until he produces the mince pies for Twelfth Night. If you stay, I promise that I expect nothing more than conversation from you and help in finishing the cake." He held out his hand to her and she knew he was offering her some apology for bedding her.

Elizabeth stood and accepted his offer, and something changed within her at that moment. Some lightening of her spirit for the first time in a very, very long time. The urge to smile won out and she felt one spread over her face. His eyes were alight with a mischievous look that promised an unforgettable meal, at the least.

Gavin felt his heart fill with hope when she smiled and stood, taking the hand he offered her and joining him at the table again. Torn now between fulfilling Orrick's request and learning more about her for some need of his own, he decided to simply let the rest of the evening happen. He was certain she would talk of personal things, of her family or her upbringing, so he could discover the information that Orrick sought.

He watched as she cleared away some of their uneaten food and moved the platters on the table aside. Once he took his seat, she served them, cutting slices of the cake he mentioned and placing it before him. Before she sat, she poured cider into two metal mugs and carried them over to the hearth. Lifting the poker from the side of the flames, she dipped it into each mug, heating the cider and releasing the fragrant aroma of apples into the air. Finally, although he knew but a few minutes had passed by, they were sitting at the table enjoying the cook's work.

"Tell me of your wife."

"My wife?" he asked, startled by her direct question.

"Aye, my lord. You mentioned that she passed away three years ago. Did she visit Lord Orrick's holding with you?"

He drank of the cider and smiled as he thought of Nessa. "Nay, she did not travel this far with me."

"Where did she travel with you?" Elizabeth maintained an even expression, nothing but honest curiosity there in her eyes. It could not hurt to talk of it, of her.

"Her family was a clan distant from mine and we traveled back to her home from time to time. Less after the children were born."

"You have children?" Her voice hinted of envy.

"I, we, have three, now all grown with bairns of their own. A daughter and two sons." Could it be this easy? "And you? Have you any bairns?"

She paled a bit at his question and shook her head rather than speaking the words. He watched as she lifted her mug to her mouth and drank deeply from it, all the time averting her eyes. The issue of children caused her some amount of pain and she tried to avoid it. Fine.

"Where—" she began, and paused when the trembling in her voice was so apparent. "Where is your village, my lord? I know only that you hail from the Highlands."

"My village is on the west coast of Scotland, about five days' ride north of Oban."

"Is it a large place?" She broke off a piece of the cake and his gaze followed her hand as it moved to her mouth.

His own mouth went dry when he saw the tip of her tongue reach out to claim the morsel. He swallowed before being able to reply.

"The entire holding is larger than Orrick's lands, but that includes all the lands held in the name of our clan. My nephew, the earl, is chief of the clan."

He thought he heard some measure of bitterness in his voice, but he did not begrudge his nephew the position he held. He supported the elders' decision to name Alasdair as chief and laird of the clan. Hell, he was one of the elders who had voted for Alasdair's claim.

"I apologize, my lord, for I cannot remember all the lessons taught by my grandmam. If your nephew rules the clan, what do you do?"

Nothing.

The word echoed through his thoughts, but he kept it within him. That was the root of his time spent here in England. Long the strongest warrior of the clan, Gavin knew he had been replaced by those younger and stronger, including his own sons. Now he served as one of the council of *elders*. That word was bitter on his tongue. Better to say the truth—he was unneeded.

He looked across and realized she was waiting for an answer, one that he did not want to say. Could not say without a further explanation he was unwilling to give. He would use her tactic.

"What did your grandmam say that you do remember?"

She looked away for a moment and then smiled. He

was beginning to enjoy the light in her eyes when she allowed a smile to grace her features.

"She often spoke of 'First Footing'? Or am I saying that wrong? She had the Gaelic and her accent was so strong that I know I am mistaken in how I remember some of the words."

He laughed out then, enchanted by the way she named his language. "You have it right, lass. On the first night, it is the custom that foretells your luck in the coming year."

"Tell me more, for I remember not the details of it."

He leaned back in the chair and finished his cider. "The age and coloring of the person who takes the first step through your doorway when midnight has passed and the gifts they bring determine how lucky and how prosperous your household will be for the next year. Many will offer coin or rewards to make certain that the 'best' person takes that first step."

"And the best to enter first?" she asked.

"Tall, dark-haired men, young and strong enough to protect those inside from those would attack and pillage."

"My lord, who would attack your village?"

"Most likely be another Scots clan on the attack, since the Norsemen keep to their isles off the coast. But the custom began long ago when they would still rampage on the mainland."

"I think my grandparents met through First Footing. He had dark hair in his youth, she said. But the memories are so hazy and long forgotten, I cannot be certain."

Their eyes met for a brief second and he was nearly knocked over by the desire for her that pulsed through him. He wanted her. And he wanted her to know it was him when he filled her. He grew hard as his body understood the feeling within him.

Wanting.

Needing.

Hunger.

She flinched. He did not believe she even knew she had done so, but he saw it and recognized that it was a reaction to him and to the lust he knew showed on his face.

Gavin stood and she sat unmoving, as though waiting to see what his intentions were. He had no doubt that if he picked her up and dragged her to the bed again, she would allow it. Or if he ordered her to take off her clothes and get into the bed on her own volition, she would do that, too. Although his body urged him to that taking, he controlled himself, not wanting to lose the meager ground he had gained since he'd used her badly earlier.

"Will you stay the night, lass?" he asked, both hoping and fearing her answer.

She blinked several times and looked at the bed before answering. "Is it your wish, my lord?" He could see her losing color and becoming empty even as she asked.

"Elizabeth, I erred when I took you without thought. I promise it will not happen again between us." Surprise, fear, resignation and puzzlement filled her eyes as she took in his words. He reached up and touched her cheek with the back of his hand. "Stay or go, it is your decision."

49

She stood and stepped away from the table. "Will you have me punished if I choose to leave?" Fear overtook the other emotions clear in her expression. She had moved just out of his reach with the steps she took toward the door. A defensive move.

"Have you been punished before for refusing?" He knew that Orrick could not have mistreated her, but who had? He took a step toward her.

"Aye, my lord, but, pray, think not that I have suffered ill treatment by Lord Orrick or his people."

But someone else had. She gave him more clues to her history even though she said little.

"Fear not, Elizabeth. I know well that Orrick does not abuse his people. And your decision to leave tonight will not be met with anything save regret on my part."

She nodded and turned to the door. He had spoken her choice and so there was nothing else to say. He did not move as she tugged the door open and walked out, pulling it closed quietly behind her. He half expected her to come back, but when several minutes passed by, he gave up any hope of it.

Unable to waste food, he took a few minutes to wrap the food that remained and could be saved. Then Gavin banked the flames in the hearth and stripped off his clothes. It took a long time for sleep to claim him that night, for his mind was filled with thoughts of her and he realized, as he drifted off, that the expression that filled her eyes called to something within him. Her vulnerability could not be ignored.

FIVE

Like insects pouring out of their nests in the ground, the inhabitants of Silloth Keep scurried forth into the bright sunlight, anxious to take advantage of the break in the near-continuous winter storms that battered the area. Defenses were strengthened, repairs made to roofs and walls damaged by the recent strong winds, and everyone who'd been cooped up for too long enjoyed the freedom, treasuring it more for not knowing how long it would last.

And preparations must be made for the upcoming festivities. Although weeks away, holly and ivy needed to be gathered to decorate the hall and, to honor Lord Orrick's heritage, a large log would be cut, carved and burned from the day of the solstice until Twelfth Night. A yule log, she was told it would be called. Under Lady Margaret's direction, groups of servants went off into the forest to accomplish those tasks.

Elizabeth finished her temporary duties under the steward's watchful eye and made her escape, as well. Her small cottage was set some distance from the keep and she had left it with no chance to prepare it for any lengthy absence. Not that she had many possessions, but she knew she would feel better checking the cottage before she was trapped in the keep once more.

The cold air knocked the breath from her as she stepped into it, but she relished the freedom from the constant company of the others and did not allow it to chase her back. Pulling her cloak tighter around her, she stepped around the many icy puddles in the yard and trotted toward the gate. The raucous yelling caught her attention and she slowed her pace, curious about what could be causing such an uproar. A crowd grew around one of the practice yards and she walked closer trying to see what was happening.

Two men, no, two warriors, of a similar size and build, fought to the cheers of the spectators around them. In spite of the cold, they had thrown off their tunics and fought in breeches alone. Sweat covered them as they struck at each other with long, wooden staffs. They were equal in ability, as well, for each spent time on the ground after being upended by his opponent. She managed to make her way closer and then recognized the combatants.

Lord Orrick.

And Lord Gavin.

He was—they were—impressive.

Although she could tell this was a friendly competition, both men were serious in their efforts. Their muscles strained as they took blows meant to knock them to the ground. Their breathing labored from the temperature around them and from their efforts. Someone in front of her turned and saw her and then moved from her path and Elizabeth was able to approach the fence surrounding the yard.

'Twas as she had thought—he was magnificent in battle. He called out his battle cry as he attacked Lord Orrick and she shivered from the fierceness of it. This could not be the same man who met her resistance with little reaction. Then, as though he'd heard her thoughts, he turned and saw her. She could not breathe.

Lord Orrick used this momentary distraction to his advantage and, before Elizabeth could blink, he struck a blow that landed Lord Gavin in the freezing mud on the ground. Laughing, Lord Orrick declared himself the winner and held out a hand to his friend.

She had cost him this battle. She had caused a lapse in his focus. How would he react to this very public embarrassment? Surely, he could not let it go unnoticed?

Not willing to wait for his reaction, Elizabeth backed away and turned toward the gate, escape the only thing on her mind. A few minutes at a quick pace took her through the gate and nearer to her cottage. Out of breath when she arrived, she lifted the latch and stepped inside. Unwilling to let the door slam against the wall, she struggled to pull it closed behind her.

The cottage was as she had left it, nothing looked out of place. First, she loosened the leather flap that covered the small cut window and then, with flint and tinder, she lit a small lamp and made a closer inspection. There were really only two things she needed to check and they were hidden in the wall near the small hearth. With an ease born of practice, she pried a stone free and reached behind it for the small box she kept within. It was still there. Elizabeth was about to take the box out when the pounding on the door came.

"Mistress Elizabeth?" a voice called out. A man's voice. "Are you within?"

Had someone followed her already? Elizabeth pushed the stone back in place. She knew that many were restless from the days and nights of inactivity within the keep, but she had no idea that someone would follow her this soon.

Going to the door, she held on to it as she opened it a crack to see who stood beyond. The miller's son. He must have seen her leave the keep and followed her. From his shifting stance and heated glances, she knew his intent. Sighing with resignation, she pushed the door open more to allow him entrance. The loud cracking of dead branches behind him drew their attention. They both looked to see the cause of the noise.

Clean, but still damp from the hurried washing he must have taken, Lord Gavin wore his hair pulled back from his face and his tunic lay stuck to his wet skin. And he stared at her with a frightening intensity that she could do no more than meet. And barely that. The miller's son understood the message. The nobleman was staking his claim. Liam stumbled back, with a tug on his forelock and an excuse to leave, and in a moment they were alone.

"My lord," she said, stepping back for him to enter. Elizabeth watched his expression as he passed her, trying to decide if he was angry or not. He had promised last night that he would not take her against her will, so why had he followed her here? Was he angry over her distraction that caused him to lose the battle with Lord Orrick?

Lord Gavin ducked to clear the low door and crossed the width of her cottage in three paces. It had never seemed as bare and mean as it did now with his presence. He filled the room and her meager possessions shrank next to him. He surveyed the room, taking it in and then turned to her.

"Did you enjoy the match?" she asked. He stood with his legs apart and his hands on his hips. She waited to listen to his tone and see if she could decipher anything from it.

"'Twas good to get some action in with Orrick after so many days within the keep."

"You were even in skills, my lord. I have seen Lord Orrick fight before, but not with one who matched him so closely in size and ability."

He turned his head and stared out the window, apparently watching the continued retreat of Liam through the trees. "It felt good. 'Twould seem we are all restless." He looked back. "Orrick said the old ones are predicting the storm's return."

"'Tis the pattern of winters here, or so I've been told, my lord." She gripped her hands together, not certain of what to do. This casual conversation was difficult to maintain. Not that she was not trained to it. Not that she did not have experience in it. But she had put that as firmly away from her as she had the contents of the hidden box. Or, rather, it had been taken from her as so many other parts of her life had been.

He relaxed a bit in his stance and smiled.

"Ah, I forget that this is your first winter in Silloth. How does this compare to your home?"

Although his probing was gently done, she felt the jab and sting of it. Swallowing to clear her throat, she needed to look away before she could answer. Would the pain be as evident in her voice as it would in her eyes?

"Silloth is my home, my lord." His questions were becoming more difficult to evade.

"'Tis now, but we each come from somewhere else. In my village," he said as he walked closer to her, "we have the same kinds of storms, but more often in winter 'tis snow instead of this rain."

"Is your village in the mountains?"

A smile tugged at the corners of his mouth and she fought the urge to touch his lips. Why was something as simple as a smile so attractive and dangerous on this man? In spite of not wearing a cloak and in spite of being wet, heat poured off him as he approached. Not until she felt the wall at her back did she realize she had backed away as he stepped closer. Now, 'twas no place left to move.

"My village sits in the valley, with mountains surrounding us. Their height protects us from many of the worst storms, but every season there are a few storms that sweep down on us." He reached out and brushed the hair that had been loosened by the winds from her face. "But we Scots do not coddle our villagers like they are wee bairns. We do not all run for cover as the weak English do." His voice trailed off to a whisper as he stroked her cheek and then her neck. "Aye, the English are too soft."

She knew he was going to kiss her. His hand crept around her neck and he steadied her for his touch. His mouth was hot, his lips firm against hers. He cupped her chin with his other hand and kissed her over and over, slanting his mouth on hers and then tasting her deeply. She thought he was done when he lifted his mouth from hers, but he simply angled it the other way and joined their mouths once more.

His presence, his body leaning against hers was overwhelming, yet she did not feel threatened. For a moment, a brief moment, she decided to simply let the sensations come. When she would have closed off her mind to what would follow, she stayed with him, staring into his eyes as he made her feel what she never permitted herself to feel.

An ache built within her at his gentle touch. Her breasts swelled as her body readied itself for what would happen next. Her hands, clenched at her sides, crept up to clasp his tunic and he pulled her closer, his arms moving down to embrace her. Still, she did not let her mind run from him. He trailed hot, wet kisses down onto her neck and then to her ear where she could have sworn he used his teeth on the sensitive skin there. Shivers passed through her and when she felt the urge to surrender to the need within her, she knew it was over.

Finally, and almost with regret, Elizabeth began the pulling away from within. Her body became a separate thing that he could use without touching her soul. It had to be this way or she would never survive the life she had to face.

Almost immediately, he released her and stepped away. His expression was intense and his breathing labored. She could smell his maleness, his strength, his desire. He was completely dangerous to her and there was nothing she could do to resist him. His displeasure screamed to her although he said nothing for a few moments.

"Why did you do that, lass?"

Elizabeth shook her head, trying to clear her thoughts. "Do what, my lord?"

"Make yourself into that lifeless thing. Why do you bundle yourself up within yourself?"

Her eyes narrowed and the frown that marred her brow told him he had hit the mark. She drew everything she was inside and left only some lifeless shell there to suffer the touches she could do nothing to prevent.

"Is it just me or do you do this with every man you lie with?"

Fear filled her expression and was tinged with something like regret. So, 'twas done apurpose. "My lord, I cannot—"

"Cannot what, Elizabeth? Lie with a man and enjoy it? Give some measure of response to his efforts? Not allow yourself to be given, but only taken?"

"I pray you, my lord," she said, raising a hand to him in a plea to stop. "Please do not make me speak of this. I beg you—" Her voice now shook as her eyes filled with tears.

'Twas the first time he knew she felt something deeply. And the conniving, questing part within him knew she would talk to him of other things if he did not force this subject now. Cursing himself for even thinking of the tactic, he asked her the question she had ignored before.

"So, how does this weather compare with that of your home?"

She took a deep breath before she replied, and they both knew she would answer him now. Part of him was exultant as she spoke the words he wanted to hear. And the other part of him felt like a bloody bastard for doing it.

"We had cold and snow in York, my lord, but not so much rain as here in Silloth."

He nodded as she revealed this truth about herself. Now he had some piece of her. Was there more? Dare he ask another? He would ask her nothing too personal that would scare her away.

"When were you last in York, Elizabeth?"

She looked away from him. "Nigh to two years have passed since I was last in York, my lord."

Defeat filled her voice and he knew she had given up resisting his questions. Gavin knew if he asked, she would answer. If he took her, she would ... be taken.

Regret for gaining knowledge of her in this manner burned within him. He was doing the same to her, again, that others did. That this time involved words and not flesh made no difference—and he knew it. He could not carry out this task for Orrick. He knew it now.

"Come, lass. Gather up what belongings you wish to take to the keep and come with me." Gavin stepped back and walked away from her. "Orrick has ordered everyone back to the keep until there is a true clearing." He reached up and pulled the leather covering over the window tightly and secured it with a sturdy knot.

"And if I do not wish to return with you? If I wish to remain here and wait out any more storms?"

Her chin rose a bit, showing a hint of defiance. She must not think that showing such to him endangered her. Or did she not know that such defiance shown to other lords in other places would garner a whipping at the least?

He picked up her cloak from the bench and held it out to her. "Even I quake in fear when Orrick wears the expression he did when he ordered everyone who had escaped back into the safety of the yard and keep. He will not be gainsaid in this order, lass."

A different sort of resignation filled her face as she accepted the cloak and threw it over her shoulders. He followed her gaze as it moved over the few furnishings in the cottage and then to the door. He had not realized how empty it was until just then. Did she have need of anything? Was there something he could do to give her ease?

Where had that thought come from? He shook his head and unlatched the door, holding on to it so it would not slam in the wind. She followed him wordlessly out of the cottage and watched him as he bolted the door with the outside latch. The whole croft had the look that a really strong wind would not force open the door but batter down the whole thing. She needed a home of sturdy stone to protect her from this kind of storm. Another ridiculous thought! Being trapped inside for all these days was making him daft.

"Come, lass, give me your hand."

He thought that holding on to her in the high winds was a good idea. As slight as she was, she could also blow or stumble away. She hesitated only for a moment and then held out her hand to him. Gavin took it in his and began walking toward the keep, tugging her along the path through the trees. When the buffeting of those treacherous winds slowed their pace, he put his arm around her waist, pulled her closer and urged her to move faster. Finally the gate to the yard came into view and he realized that she had dug her heels into a soft place in the frozen mud around them.

"My lord, please go on without me. I need to catch my breath." She twisted to free herself from his grasp and he released her as soon as he realized it. He understood something else, as well.

"Do you fear that others will talk if we are seen together here?"

"Fear it, my lord? Nay. 'Tis a fact already and a topic of gossip throughout Silloth and its people."

"They gossip about us? Why would they do such a thing?" Why would such a thing as speaking to her or having her help with his bath bring them to the center of attention? 'Twas her duties to do so at his request. But he was not so dull witted that he did not know that in the dead of winter, there was not any small bit of activity that went unnoticed or unmentioned in the closeness of living in a keep.

"Was it not your aim, then? You did not intend to stake your claim of me while you are here visiting Lord Orrick? To keep the other men away?"

"Nay," he protested, and it sounded too loud and too fervent to even his own ears. "I did no such thing!"

"I suspect, my lord, that you are the only one in Silloth who missed the intent of your actions. Or is it your intention to simply toy with me until you tire of whatever draws you to me?" She stood with her hands fisted on her hips and let the anger that had obviously been building within her pour forward. "Then you will take your pleasure and move on to the next woman who catches your fancy. So, tell me, my lord, do I resist too much or not enough for your tastes? Tell me so I may get through these games you play with me."

She gasped and a look of horror covered her face as the words escaped her. Gavin knew that even if she had been known as a bold wench, she had just crossed the line to arrogance. And it was a line that should be met with a reprimand or punishment severe enough that she would not think herself better or smarter than those superior to her in standing and in rights. Elizabeth stumbled back a few steps as if she expected him to mete out what her impudence had earned.

And he was horrified, as well, at her words, but not because they insulted his position. Not even because, as a serf tied to this land and to this lord, she had no right to object to anything her lord's guest said or did, whether it was to her or to another.

Gavin was horrified because her words were true.

He could think of nothing to say to her, so he stepped back and walked away, leaving her to remain behind as she had asked—alone to enter the keep by herself. This game of Orrick's had gotten out of hand and he did not know how to bring it back under his control. However, Gavin knew too well that he must.

He trotted toward the gate, but instead of entering the yard, he followed a path to the cliff's edge where he could see the high waves of the sea bashing their fury on the beach. Gavin grasped the rough rock of the outer wall to keep from slipping down the steep trail that led down to the beach. The winds were even stronger here than in the woods and, as he watched, storm clouds darkened and gathered off to the west. The old ones were right— this was but a temporary reprieve in the storm. Knowing that far more important tasks needed to be handled before the storm was back on them, Gavin decided to put his soul-searching aside for another time. He would have words with Orrick and settle this.

SIX

"This game of yours ends now, my friend. I will play no longer and get caught in the web you weave around me."

He slammed the door to Orrick's chamber and stood in front of it, awaiting his friend's reaction. Orrick stood by one of the glazed windows in the wall, looking out. Gavin strode over to his side and watched as the rains began pelting the villagers who had not yet sought cover in the keep. Orrick did not answer him, so Gavin prodded him again.

"I am leaving for home when there is a real break in the weather. I fear I have lost the desire to stay here until Twelfth Night is upon us."

"Did you know that I can see to the southern tree line from this window?"

With a sinking feeling, Gavin pushed to where Orrick stood and looked out. She still stood there, alone, as the rains poured over her. If she felt the cold or wet, he knew not, for she did not move. Her arms were wrapped around herself, but she gave no other indication of being alive.

He shifted his stance, calling out to her in his thoughts to get inside and out of the worsening weather. Just as he reached the limit of his patience, she came alive, looking around and then rushing toward the gate. He let out his breath.

"You have learned something disquieting about Elizabeth? Is that what troubles you, Gavin?" Orrick handed him a cup of ale. "Tell me what you've discovered about her."

Gavin swallowed deeply of the brew and thought about the question. He had discovered more about himself and his own limits than he had about the young woman. He had learned that he did not use people as easily as some could—mayhap that was why he was better at battle than at subterfuge and strategy. He learned that he was willing to help a friend, but he could not harm an innocent in carrying out the task. And she was an innocent, he had no doubt.

And Gavin had learned that he could indeed fall in love twice in his life.

The metal cup was crushed in his grasp as the truth of it punched him in the gut. For all that Gavin claimed that Orrick coddled his people, Gavin knew that he had the softer heart. And that Elizabeth, with her ingrained innocence and vulnerability, had claimed it. What the hell did he do now? In love with the village whore? What kind of a daft lackwit was he?

"Gavin?" Orrick's soft question invaded his thoughts.

"She hails from York, although she has not been there

for nigh on two years. I suspect she was gentle or noble born but mayhap on the wrong side of the blanket. And," he added, "I believe she cannot survive the life she is living for much longer."

"Has she threatened to take her life again? She swore to me that she would not pursue that again if I gave her a place here." Orrick's face paled. Suicide was the most grievous sin a soul could commit; even discussing it was uncomfortable.

Gavin considered his options. He could simply ignore what he felt and blame it on his friend's foolish quest. He could stay here and get to know her better and discover if she felt anything at all for him. He could…he shook his head and glared at his friend.

"Did you know I would fall in love with her when you put your plan in motion? Or was I just a respite you thought to offer her during this slow time of the year? An old fool who would never force her to her back?"

"It may surprise you to know that 'twas my ladywife who first suggested that you might be a match for each other."

"Is this some joke, then? Putting together the English whore and Scots outcast?" He slammed the now-empty cup down on the table near the blazing hearth and turned to his host. "Two misfits who have no place in the world and deserve none."

Orrick did not rush to an answer. Instead, he walked to a chair and sat in it, drinking his own ale leisurely. Then he faced Gavin.

"Is that how you see yourself? An outcast? Your clan values your service and…"

"Bah! I am an old man who has outlived his usefulness. My sons fight in my place. My nephew rules as he pleases. There is nothing left for me there." Gavin felt the bile rise in his stomach. He had thought these notions before, but this was the first time he had voiced them to anyone.

"So, should I have the tailor prepare your shroud? Will you lie down and die now or linger until someone puts you out of your misery?" Orrick's sarcasm bit deeply. "You are worse than a woman, bemoaning that which cannot be changed. In all the time that fate has dealt Elizabeth the cruel life it has, never did I hear her complain as you do now."

Gavin grabbed Orrick's tunic and dragged him to stand before forcing him up against the wall. Thumping his head once more against the stone, Gavin growled through clenched jaws.

"How do you dare to say such things to me? I should have taken no pity on you today and crushed you in the dirt as you deserve." He shoved Orrick again and then released him. Pacing away from him, Gavin poured more ale and drank it down. Orrick stayed on the other side of the room.

"It is widely known that no decision is made in the clan MacLeod without your voice being heard. Your nephew credits you with enlarging and protecting the lands under his control. Be at peace about your value to your people."

When he would argue, Orrick held up his hand to stop him. "If you doubt that you still have a place there, then you are welcome here. I would appreciate your help in keeping my lands safe and my properties maintained and successful."

Staying was a choice.

He and Orrick had worked well for many years in various endeavors and they had protected each other's backs more times than he could count. But what would happen to Elizabeth? He wanted her. He wanted her very much, with such a hunger that it made him uneasy.

"And Elizabeth?" he asked. "What would become of her if I stayed here?"

"I have been thinking of sending her to Margaret's niece near Carlisle."

"The nun?" he asked, stunned at the thought. "You would have her enter a convent?"

"The Gilbertines maintain a lay community as well as their religious order. Mayhap Elizabeth could find some measure of peace there."

Orrick's suggestion was a good one. The convent offered protection to women who had no place in the world. She would not need to earn her living on her back.

"I would marry her if she would have me."

Orrick gasped at his declaration and Gavin wondered when the idea had formed in his mind. He could do worse. She was young enough but not so young. He could protect her and offer her a place to live. The glimpses of personality hiding beneath layers of fear would shine through with some encouragement and tolerance. His needs were not the same now as when he had married Nessa, and the unexpected love he felt for Elizabeth was very different from the burning, naive passions of youth.

"I fear that would cause some problems. Margaret, as tolerant as she is and as much as she might want to, would never accept her at table or in her company. None of her ladies would. It is something else completely for my ladywife to be asked to ignore the situation when an honored guest has needs and desires, then to be expected to welcome the village harlot into her circle."

Gavin knew this. He knew it well. No matter what Elizabeth's true beginnings were, the past months spent here were lived as a whore and she would be remembered as such. Although he thought himself able to look beyond that as long as it was over, he knew that society's rules were more stringent than that. Everyone had a place, knew it and kept to it. 'Twas the way God ordained it to be.

Only a fool questioned or tried to change that. Only a fool or a man foolishly loving where he should not. Right now, he knew only that he was one of those, but did not have the slightest clue which he was.

"Think on this before you act, friend. Many lives will be changed by whatever path you take." Orrick stood and looked at him with grim eyes. "I fear I made a mistake when I challenged you about her." A soft knock on the door caught their attention. "She comes now at my call."

"And you will tell her what? Of the quest that I began to uncover her secrets?" Gavin knew how closely she guarded anything about herself and her past and the comment she had flung at him outside the gate was so close to the truth that it would hurt her immensely to find out how near. And he did not want to hurt her.

Orrick walked past him to the door and put his hand on the knob. "I will remind her of the bargain she made with me and make her choices clear once more."

Before he could ask anything else, Orrick pulled open the door, revealing Lady Margaret with Elizabeth standing off to one side and behind her. The women entered and their silent stances told Gavin clearly that he was the outsider here. 'Twas best to retreat and regroup. So, as he bowed courteously to his friend's wife and strode past Elizabeth, he could not help but whisper in her ear, "Come to me, Elizabeth. Please."

His heated breath near her ear sent shivers down and through her and Elizabeth trembled from the ardor in his words and tone. That it caused such a reaction scared her and warned her of the weakness developing in the walls she had laboriously built around herself.

Then she remembered her words to Lord Gavin and realized he and Lord Orrick must have discussed her. She had insulted him, and in doing so, insulted the man before her now, who had shown her only mercy and concern. She must apologize. Dragging her sopping cloak along with her, she waited for Lady Margaret to finish their exchange of words and then she fell to her knees before them both and leaned her head down further in as complete a gesture of obeisance as she could make.

"My lord. My lady. I beg your forgiveness for my actions toward your guest." Elizabeth stayed on her knees with her head bowed, awaiting their words.

"What did you do to Lord Gavin?" Lady Margaret's voice was soft, but in no way less powerful for the gentleness of it.

"I refused his attentions and insulted his honor."

"'Twould be easier to speak to you if your face was not on the floor. Would you stand so I can hear your words?"

Elizabeth gasped and then hurried to comply with the lady's request. She had already left a puddle of water around her from her garments so she placed her cloak on it to soak up some of it. She was about to begin her apology again, when Lord Orrick spoke.

"The reprieve from the storm was not as long as everyone had hoped and you are one of many who was caught by the onslaught of rain. Stand here." He pointed to a place closer to where he stood. "The heat from the hearth cannot reach you there."

If the lady thought it strange for her husband to be offering comfort to a whore, she gave no indication by her expression or manners. Elizabeth knew this was not the way in most noble households. To be given a private interview by the lord and lady, instead of hearing their decisions and orders through several layers of servants and retainers, was quite unusual. She moved to the place he had designated and repeated her words. "I am sorry for refusing and insulting your guest, my lord." She bowed her head and did not meet either of their gazes.

"He most likely deserved the insults," Lady Margaret said.

"And the refusal," Lord Orrick added.

"Did you insult his manners or his place of origin? His manners were probably the safer target. These Scots do not like their customs and families called into question," the lady said.

"As long as you did not insult his fighting abilities, he will not take it seriously." Lord Orrick laughed out loud then, and his wife joined in with him.

Elizabeth looked up in shock. They thought this amusing? She had dared to even speak when not asked something and they were defending her? Even counseling her on how to insult their guest. She knew that her mouth dropped open and she was staring, but she could not stop herself.

"Elizabeth, what think you of Lord Gavin?"

Her breath held in her chest and no words would form in answer to her lord. What did she think of Gavin MacLeod of the Scots? So many things.

He was arrogant and proud and fearless and hard and strong. He was thoughtful and did not let his cock make his decisions, at least not most of the time. He listened to her and showed concern for her safety and comfort. He lusted for her yet controlled it and did not force her to something she did not want. Well, only the once and she was not certain why he had lost control of himself then. He was…he was….

"Forgive me, my lord, but he is peculiar."

"He is a Scot, after all," Lady Margaret added as though that explained it clearly.

Lord Orrick laughed again and then his expression turned serious. "'Twould seem the time to remind you of our agreement, Elizabeth."

"My lord?" Did he mean to turn her out of Silloth for her transgressions against his friend? Surely not. She tried to search her memories for the words they exchanged when he held her back from stepping off the edge of the cliff that day many months ago.

"I told you that you could remain with us here in Silloth until you were ready to make the choice to live."

She began to shake, the desperation and desolation of that day pouring over her. She had been wandering for days, weeks, with little food or water or shelter or even sleep. Moving from one horror to another to simply survive, Elizabeth had found herself on the road just outside the village. Knowing what most villagers did to itinerant whores, she walked away from the village, drawn by the fresh smell of the nearby ocean. Her steps led her to the cliff wall, not far from the keep.

How long she had stood staring at the powerful waves crashing onto the rocks below her, she knew not. The wind had torn at her thin skirt and threadbare cloak and pulled her hair loose from the kerchief she had wrapped around it. She closed her eyes and took a deep breath.

One step.

Just one step more and all the pain would be gone. She would whore for no one again. She would give up her immortal soul, but the peace of that terrible choice called to her.

But could she? Was she not already being punished for her sins? Was escaping this misery truly worth an eternity of damnation?

One step remained.

She still did not know if she had lifted her foot to take the step or not, but Orrick's strong arm around her waist prevented her from falling. The next thing she remembered was waking up warm and dry for the first time in months. Orrick and Silloth had offered her sanctuary and she had accepted it. But not without paying a price.

"Elizabeth?" His deep voice pierced through her reverie and she blinked several times until the fog of that time cleared.

"Aye, my lord?" She realized that her throat had gone dry, so she swallowed several times to loosen it. "What choice is that?"

"We know not why you have chosen to punish yourself in this way, but 'twas not ours to question. But you have changed now, recovered from your condition when you arrived and grown stronger in these last weeks. 'Tis time to make a choice."

"What choice do I have, my lord. My lady?" she asked. "You are lord here and decide these matters. I owe you much and would do as you say."

"'Tis the season of Our Lord's Birth and a time to reexamine our lives, Elizabeth," the lady said quietly. "Lord Orrick would sponsor you in the spring to live with my niece at the Gilbertine convent near Carlisle if you wish it. You could live and work in their lay community, or, if you feel the Lord's call, take your vows and live with the good sisters there."

"Or you could stay here," Lord Orrick added. "But if you do, you must do other work."

Other work? But she was a whore. What else was she good enough to do? Good people would not associate with her, afraid that her filth would spread onto them or corrupt them as it had corrupted her. No, she shook her head. Those were her father's words, not hers.

When she began to argue with him, he raised his hand to stop her. "You have told me none of your past, but even I can see that you were raised to another life. I can see the pain and guilt in your eyes every time someone calls you 'whore.'" He paused and took Lady Margaret's hand in his and they met her gaze as one. "But we know the untruth of it, even if you will not admit it to us or to yourself."

Her body began to tremble on its own, violently as the cold and wet clothing enveloped her in their chill. Whether caused by their words or her own fears, she knew not. But once it started, the tremors would not stop.

Lady Margaret walked past her to the door and pulled it open, whispering orders to someone outside. Soon a blanket was wrapped around her shoulders and she was being guided from the chamber by one of Lady Margaret's serving women.

"You must change or you will take a chill. Go with Lynna and do as she says."

"But, my lord—" She looked back to Orrick, who stood simply observing his wife's direction of the scene around them. "He has summoned me. Lord Gavin has—"

"He invited you as a woman, Elizabeth, not as a whore who answers at his beck and call. Do as you will."

His words did not make any sense to her. What was the difference? Lord Gavin wanted her in a way that made her skin tingle and in a way that tempted her to say yes.

"I do not understand, my lord. My lady?"

Lynna was guiding her out of the room as Lord Orrick answered.

"And neither does he, Elizabeth. Neither does he."

SEVEN

It took two days for her to build up her courage and make her decision. Lady Margaret's servant seemed to find things for her to do that gave her time to think and that kept her out of view from most of the keep's inhabitants. Well, if the truth were told, Lady Margaret insured that she did not see Lord Gavin during this time. And that he did not find her. Elizabeth did not know if he even sought her out but suspected from the fervor in his invitation that he might have.

Her choice to go to the Gilbertine community was not a difficult one at all. Lord Orrick's sponsorship and the word of Lady Margaret was more than enough for her to be permitted to join their community. She did not think she would take vows, for 'twould take much in penance and prayer to cleanse her soul from her many transgressions. If she did decide she heard the call, her mother's jeweled ring, safely hidden in her cottage, would be enough to pay the dowry required.

She felt stronger somehow in making the decision and

knowing that she would choose her path. That knowledge did not lessen the gratitude she owed to and felt toward the lord and lady of Silloth. Orrick could have claimed her as a serf and forced her to belong to him as part of his demesne. No one would have or could have challenged his right to that. But he never did. One more extraordinary thing to be thankful for.

Now she walked slowly up the steps and down the corridor that led to Lord Gavin's chamber. Standing quietly outside his door, she thought on this once more. If she was leaving the world behind, she needed to be with him before she did. His embraces and his kisses were the only ones that had ever promised her something and made her want whatever that was. Her body had reacted to the touch of many men, but her heart and soul had stirred only at his. As she reached to knock, she prayed that he would not refuse her this small favor.

Elizabeth heard him moving within the chamber and waited for him to open the door. It shouldn't have, but his appearance surprised her. He opened the door from behind it and she knew from his stance that he was naked and that he held his sword at the ready. His real sword. His eyes widened and then he opened the door to let her enter. As she moved into the room, he tugged on his breeches behind the door before closing it.

"Old habit, I fear," he said, nodding toward the sword that lay on the floor near the door. "I expected no visitors this night."

She had considered what her words should be for

hours before she approached his door, but all of the well-practiced ones disappeared as she met his hungry gaze. Were words even necessary? She would not burden someone of his status with words of love. She could not give them and he could not accept them or the promise that was always at the core of them. He would understand the significance of her presence here and her actions in offering herself to him.

They stood several paces apart. Pure terror kept her from taking the first step toward him. So many things were wrong with this; so many things could go wrong. Deep inside, Elizabeth knew he would not let it, and so she made the first movement. 'Twas just a small one, not a step at all, but as she did, he opened his arms to her and she was in his embrace and surrounded by his strength in but a moment.

Not sure what to expect, she waited. Would it be as quick as that other time? Would he linger as some men did, intent on evoking something from her body as he took his pleasure? Would he take her? How could she do this?

She could not breathe. Elizabeth struggled against his hold, trying to pull air into her chest. He did not loosen his grasp and she felt as though the world were going dark. Just before it did, he released her. As her legs gave out, he scooped her up and carried her to the bed. After placing her there, he poured two cups of ale and made her drink some of hers.

"Do not try to talk, lass. Just drink this all. And breathe."

The nervous look on her face had turned to terror just as she reached him and it took only a moment before her struggles became apparent to him. As much as he would have liked to keep her in his arms, just knowing that she was here was enough to give him the courage to let her go. Gavin watched as she emptied the cup and handed it back to him.

"So, I am back to being the terrifying Scots warrior now? You fear my strength and size again?" He tried to keep some measure of levity in his voice and it must have worked, for she gifted him with a soft smile.

"As my grandmam would say," she began.

He laughed. "I am certain not to like what she said, so let us move on to something more pleasant." He sat down next to her so that he did not tower over her and he was pleased beyond measure when she did not move away or cringe from him.

"I… my lord… I…." She began several times and never got past the first word or two. Gavin decided that they did not need words at this time and dipped down and touched his lips to hers, silencing any more attempts to speak. When she opened her mouth and welcomed his tongue, he lost the ability to speak.

Steadying himself with a hand on each side of her, he let her grow accustomed to him before moving forward. She accepted his kisses and even when he pressed for more, she gave it.

She gave it!

Surprised by this realization, he drew back and searched her face, her eyes, for some explanation.

"I have only done this as a whore, my lord. I know not how to do this any other way." Tears glistened in her eyes and his heart hurt as he knew that she was offering him something very precious indeed.

"And I have only done this as a husband for a very long time, lass. Mayhap we can show each other the way?"

His words sank in and a stab of pain pierced him. He had given her a truth that had not been known to him before that moment. Oh, he had lain with other women since Nessa's death, but those times had never involved his heart. Or his soul. This time with Elizabeth did and now they both knew it. When he almost drew back from her to let the pain pass, her soft hands touched his face, holding his cheeks and bringing his mouth back to hers.

That small gesture broke through any hesitation either of them had and he pressed her back onto the pillows as he claimed her mouth with his. He wanted nothing so much as to fill the softness he knew would now welcome him, but he fought to keep his desires under control until she was ready. Until she took him. If she could. He lay on his side, and she turned to meet his mouth again.

Gavin tasted her deeply and tugged up the length of her gown and the chemise under it up until he could touch her bare skin. The shudder that went through her simply intensified the arousal he was feeling and he grew harder than he had been. He thought she might be ticklish when she squirmed at his light stroking of her knee and then he moved his hand onto the soft skin of her inner thighs. When her legs opened, he drew back to look into her eyes. If they were empty as before, he would go no further.

She returned his gaze with wide eyes. Not sure if they were wide with fear or anticipation, he slid his hand up until it grazed the silky hair between her legs. Then Gavin parted her woman's flesh and slipped one finger into her heated depths. He did not touch deeper but waited for her reaction. 'Twas swift in coming.

Elizabeth grabbed at his arm and seemed to want to stop him, but she licked her lips and loosened her hold. He leaned down and kissed her once more, sucking gently on her tongue as his fingers moved inside her and found the wetness and heat he desired. She moved restlessly beneath his touch and finally, finally, he felt her hand move from his arm to his chest. He paused and guided her to his hardness, hoping she would, but not forcing her to touch him. And she did.

He did not realize that he had not laced his breeches until her hand slipped inside and grasped his erection. The moan escaped him and filled her mouth before he could stop it. Her small hand and light touch teased his eager flesh and he rocked against her palm in spite of his fear that he would disgrace himself and come too quickly. For a moment, he felt like a youth instead of the aging man he was. When she slid her hand down onto his sac, he knew he must stop her.

"Elizabeth, lass," he whispered as he lifted his mouth from hers. "Can we take this off?" He tugged at her gown. "I would see all of you before we join."

However, before she could comply, she surged against his hand as he spoke and he felt the wetness pour from within her. Not wanting to miss this chance to pleasure her, he slid another finger into her and rubbed from inside out. Elizabeth arched and her eyes grew wider. Her breath had turned to panting and she was trembling next to him.

Gavin moved his other arm beneath her head and pulled her closer, trapping her leg with his thigh. He became relentless in his touch, spreading her woman's wetness over the flesh there until she gifted him with several moans. She tilted her chin and tried to lift her head to his, so he lowered his mouth to hers and mimicked the actions of his hand with his tongue. Soon he felt her body tighten and arch and he knew her peak was on her.

"My lord?" She grabbed his arm again and he read the fear in her expression. "I cannot—"

"Let go, lass," he urged. "Trust me and let go."

She closed her eyes and he thought she would refuse to let go of her control and her fear at what he was doing, but a smile tugged the corners of her mouth.

"As you wish, my lord," she murmured after a moment, her eyes now open and meeting his.

"Gavin. My name is Gavin. Say it. Please."

Now she smiled fully as she spoke. "As you wish, Gavin."

"Nay, lass." He shook his head slightly. "'Tis as you wish this time."

He made no move yet to climb on top of her and his words startled her. He sought to pleasure her first, something that had never happened before to her. Not in all the years with Kennard, not in the months and months earning her living on her back. No man had ever put her pleasure before his own.

Elizabeth felt the tightness winding within her until the tension felt too intense, too pleasurable. Even though she recognized the pull to loosen herself from what her body felt, she gave Gavin her trust and stayed with him. And the reward for it made her breathless. When she would usually feel threatened by such a close hold, she now felt cradled and safe. When she would have turned inward and shut off what she felt, she now let the enjoyment of his touch, his kiss, his pleasuring of her fill her.

Aching and throbbing from within, she moved in time with the motion of his fingers until the scream welled in her. Wound beyond tightening, she felt the waves of sensation pour over and through her and this time she let it come. Her flesh, her whole body, tingled and tensed even where he did not touch. And then, when she thought she could feel no more, she fell.

And Gavin caught her.

It took a few minutes for her to catch her breath and in that time, he never stopped touching her. His hand glided soothingly over her hip and onto her stomach. He lifted her hair from her face and touched a soft kiss on her swollen lips.

She enjoyed the softer waves that still moved through her and knew that this was the bliss that could happen between a man and woman, something that she'd heard so much about but had never experienced before. She waited for him to say or do something, not sure of what would happen next.

And still he did not take her.

She knew he could, she could feel his hard flesh against her leg as they lay together on the bed. He moved neither closer to nor farther from her. Puzzled, she slid from his side and pushed herself back to sit. She still wore her gown and he his breeches, but the proof of his lack of fulfillment pushed through the gap in the breeches and she wondered if she should pleasure him now.

Before she could do or say anything, he rolled from the bed and handed her the other cup of ale he had poured before and filled the empty one for himself. She drank hers and watched over the rim as he did the same, although he turned slightly from her as he did. Elizabeth choked on the ale as she realized he was covering himself and tying the laces as he drank.

"Was that the first time you… reached your peak?" He said the words, but the wonderful blush that filled his cheeks told of his embarrassment over voicing the subject. "You seemed surprised by it, almost fearful."

How did she answer him without lying or telling him too much? Never in the times with Kennard had her pleasure been important. There were a few times when it was pleasant, but more often than not, it was a hurried affair done in the dark of night and with as little physical exertion as was needed to complete the act.

The first times at the house where she was brought into her trade were too unpleasant to think on and she did not want to ruin this experience with Gavin with memories of those times. He was waiting for an answer, watching her with those piercing blue eyes of his. She gave him the truth.

"Aye, my lord. 'Twas the first time I have felt such things."

"Great God in Heaven! What sort of men are these Sassenachs that they cannot make certain a woman is well-pleasured as they take theirs?"

He slammed down his cup and raked his hands through his hair. Then he looked at her with bleak eyes and she knew he was thinking what had happened between them on this very bed. Before he could speak again, she slid from the bed and walked to him. That had been a mistake; she knew how deeply he regretted taking her that night. He told her with words and by his actions that it had been a misjudgment on his part to do so. No other man had ever regretted his callous taking of her body as his due.

Only this one.

She stepped closer and smiled at him. She wanted to offer him something to show him how much she appreciated his thoughtfulness. She needed to show him how much she cared for him. All she had to give was herself.

Elizabeth loosened the ties on her gown and chemise, bent over and grasped the bottom of the garments and lifted them up. Luckily these were borrowed clothes from someone much bigger than she was, so she was able to get them off. Of course, Lord Gavin's hands pulling them over her head helped. She stood naked before him and waited for him to accept.

She followed his hands as they untied his laces and pushed his breeches down over his hips to the floor, exposing his powerful hips and legs to her sight. And his manhood that was still hardened and ready. He reached down and pulled the breeches free and threw them in the corner. Then he stood straight. The fire in his eyes told her he wanted her, but there was something else that reassured her.

When he took her in his arms, her skin sizzled at his touch. Their bodies met and the heat of his warmed her and made her shiver, as well. He turned around and pulled her with him to the side of the bed. Once more he surprised her by sitting on the edge of it and bringing her to stand in front of him. The soft touch of his fingertips on her breasts made her tremble and she felt her eyes close as she concentrated on how her body felt under his touch.

His mouth replaced his fingers and she gasped loudly at how quickly the tension within her built. One and then the other breast received his attentions and her breasts swelled as he suckled on them, tasting them and drawing her nipple into his mouth. When she felt the nip of his teeth against the sensitive buds, she reached out to steady herself. Her hands met his hard chest and she looked at him. Surely he did not mean to pleasure her again? Lord Gavin laughed and Elizabeth realized she'd spoken the words aloud.

"Aye, lass, 'tis my plan. But I would not be opposed if you would like to add to my pleasure." He paused and took her hand, guiding it toward his hardness.

Ah. Elizabeth knew what he wanted. Many men wanted her to take them in her mouth rather than in her body. She didn't understand it, but if it would give him pleasure, she would grant him this service. She began to kneel in front of him when his expression darkened. Something was wrong.

"Nay, Elizabeth. Do not kneel to me." He took her by the shoulders and lifted her back to her feet. "I but wanted to feel the touch of your hands there."

"Not my mouth?"

"Not if you do not want to. This is not about force now, lass. 'Tis about wanting."

She shook her head. She did not want to do that. It had been forced on her many times, but she never liked it. "I would rather not, my lord." Elizabeth waited for his reaction.

"Then let us discover what you do like to do, lass," he said, and his voice grew deep and warm. "Tell me what you think of this."

His strength amazed her as he lifted her by the hips, brought her onto his lap and slid them both back on the bed. In another moment she found herself sitting over his legs, astride him with his hardness directly under the flesh she now discovered was still quite sensitive. His hands, now freed from supporting his body over hers, explored her body, touching everywhere, making her shiver and shudder as he did.

Elizabeth felt him pulsing beneath her and knew she wanted him inside of her. Surprised that she could feel this desire for a man or for joining with a man, she sat back on his hips and looked at him. Her heart filled with love and tears burned her eyes and throat as she thought of all the years lost in her life and all the unhappiness that had come before. If only they had met before, before she had before.

He must have noticed the tears, but she was thankful he did not speak of them. Instead he urged her forward to him and brought her to the brink of pleasure with his mouth on her breasts.

"Take me, lass," he whispered to her as he kissed her. "Take me now."

He let her go and she slid back to take him inside her. The thrill of controlling this coupling made her clumsy. "Help me," she whispered as she moved back and tried to guide him into her.

He drew his knees up a bit and supported her bottom with his legs and his hands spread her woman's flesh. With little effort on her part, his hardness entered her and soon she was filled with him. He let out a moan that spoke of his pleasure. He gifted her with a wicked smile, one that foretold of even more gratification to come and then he guided her hips to move as though she were riding a horse.

Elizabeth gasped when he placed his hand between them and began to tease that place between her legs. The aching and throbbing increased every time she moved and because of the pleasure she could not stop herself. The tension built even more tightly than before within her, and she arched her back and took him in as deeply as she could. Filled with him, she moaned as she reached the edge of something and hesitated for a brief moment, before going over it.

As the core of her began to contract, he reached out and clasped her hands in his. He needed to be even deeper inside of her and so he rolled them over until he covered her. Releasing her hands, he lifted her legs around his hips and plunged his flesh in until he met her womb. As tight as the glove he wore for hawking, she fit around him, and he could feel every little pulse as it moved through her. Lifting out and then sliding back in, he filled her over and over until she began to cry out her pleasure. Only then did he seek his release, the one that he had held back until assured that she was satisfied. Until she took control.

Until she took him and was not taken.

Until she was given.

EIGHT

He knew not how long they slept, only that he awakened to find her on top of him with her hair covering them like a blanket. Although he was hot, her skin felt chilled.

There was no way to get out from under her to stir the embers of the fire or to even pull the covers over them without waking her, so he began to ease her to his side. Although she grumbled, she did not seem to wake. Gavin slipped from the bed and picked up an iron rod to stir the peat in the hearth. Adding a few more blocks of it and a few pieces of wood, Gavin looked back to where she slept.

He still could not believe that she had answered his summons. She'd made him wait for two days and almost lose hope, but then she was there. And she had given herself to him as he'd hoped. Surely they were meant to be together.

He had tried everything he knew to make it good for her, to make the memories of the other times with other men fade and to make her realize what could be between a man and a woman. Especially when deeper feelings were involved. As his were.

Elizabeth began stirring so he finished tending the hearth and returned to the bed. Easing the blankets out from under her, he climbed in and was thrilled when she rolled into his arms and murmured in her sleep. His own body stirred as her softness came into contact with him, but he simply enjoyed holding her close without her fears to get in the way.

"I love ye, lass," he whispered to her, in the Gaelic language of his home. "With all my heart."

She opened her eyes and looked at him. Before she could speak, he touched her lips with his and then smiled. "I am glad that you answered my summons, lass."

"As am I, my—" He stopped her from finishing it.

"Gavin. With all this between us now, we are Elizabeth and Gavin."

Her smile lit his world and she repeated his name in a throaty whisper. "Gavin."

"'Twas the first time you found pleasure in the joining?" he asked, not sure how else to broach the subject without asking it directly.

She looked away, obviously uncomfortable with speaking of it, but he would not let her. Guiding her face back to where he could see it, he kissed her and then asked again.

"Was it?" He was not sure why he asked. Partly male pride, partly curiosity over her past. But he needed to know.

"Not all… joinings have been pleasant, but some have been not unpleasant," she began to explain. "But none have been as was between us."

His arrogance and pride surged as did certain parts of his body at her words. She had gifted him with something precious, as he suspected. And he had been able to make it different and better for her. Did she know now that so much more could be between them? Did she know that more of herself, more than she had buried deep inside her, would be safe with him?

"And will be again, if you wish it so, lass," he said.

She leaned away from him, as far as his arms would allow and searched his face. "You wish me to stay?"

"Aye, lass. I wish you to stay." He was not about to allow her to leave. He would do whatever he must to convince her to remain with him, until he could speak to her seriously of a possible life together. "Please dinna leave me." Even he heard the longing in his voice and he offered up a silent prayer that she felt it.

"I will stay with you, Gavin, until you send me away."

She let him gather her in closer as he tried to show her with his embrace and his body that he would never ask her to leave. Just the opposite, he planned to ask her to stay with him forever.

Two more days and nights passed and still he kept her to himself. He loved her in every way possible and she never refused him. Actually, she became quite the active partner, giving and receiving until they were spent.

Gavin arranged for food and a bath to be brought and still did not allow her to leave.

'Twas only when Orrick himself banged on the door, demanding that Elizabeth return to her duties, that Gavin relented in his possession of her and hers of him. Not wishing to cause more trouble or embarrassment for her, Gavin allowed her to answer Orrick's summons.

But the Elizabeth who left his chambers was a different one than the fearful woman who had entered there a few days before. The tantalizing glimpses of the woman inside confirmed to him his suspicions that there was much more to her than a common whore. She let small clues slip out during their loveplay and in their conversations about her past, before she left York.

And her personality was strong and vibrant! She showed him a keen and sometimes biting sense of humor and an appreciation for learning his culture and heritage. The lass took a passive role in their joinings only the first two times, then she led as much as she followed, to his utter amazement and joy.

There were two things he knew clearly when she walked out of his chambers—that they would suit well and that he did love her. He suspected that she had soft feelings for him, but he did not press for words of love. They would come in time, he was certain. He had only to arrange things with Orrick and then he would ask her to return with him to his home in the Highlands. A short time after she left, he too was summoned to Orrick's presence.

Elizabeth wondered if everyone in Silloth knew what they had been doing for the past two days and nights. She ached in places she did not know existed before his touches and kisses and felt a contentment she did not know before his love.

Aye, she thought as she answered Lord Orrick's call, she knew Gavin thought he was in love with her. And, if truth be told, she would like that very much, but the true situation was not and could not be that simple...or happy. In spite of his words declaring his love, spoken in the Gaelic of her grandmother, nothing could come of it.

Convinced now more than when she went to his chambers of the rightness of her decision to enter the Gilbertines community and her decision to give herself to him before leaving Silloth, she tucked the wonderful memories of their time together into a safe place and made her way down the stairs and corridors until she stood before Orrick's chamber. Knocking, she waited to be invited in before opening the door. Lady Margaret's presence was no surprise. Elizabeth knew she had some explaining to do to both lord and lady over her behavior and her plans.

"Elizabeth, are you well?" Lady Margaret asked softly as soon as her servant left them, pulling the door closed behind her. Orrick stood off to one side of the chamber, looking out the window as if not involved. She knew better, though.

Elizabeth curtsied slightly and nodded. "I am well, my lady."

"And you discovered what you went seeking to find?" The lady's gaze missed nothing as did her knowledge of her people.

"I did, my lady."

"And did you and Lord Gavin speak of your lives after this time you spent together? What will you do?"

"I fear we *spoke* of very little, my lady." Lord Orrick choked and coughed a few times at her words, no doubt shocked at her boldness. "I would accept the offer made by you and my lord to sponsor me to the Gilbertines, my lady. I will go there whenever you think it best to go."

Now that she spoke the words, a sense of peace settled over her. This was the right path for her. For she was certain that she could never again offer herself to any man for his pleasure. Now that she had given herself to Gavin, she would not be able to resurrect the barriers that kept her safe and separate.

And she did not want to be with another man if she could not be with him. Elizabeth had given him something that she had shared with no other man and would not betray or dirty that by going back to whoring. She might be placing herself too high, but she knew the truth of it inside her heart and her soul.

"Gavin does not know of your plans?" Lord Orrick asked.

"Nay, my lord." Something was amiss here.

"And he did not speak to you of his plans?" Lord Orrick's tone hinted at something, but she did not know what.

"Nay, my lord. Was there some reason to tell him of my decision?"

"He is a fool, Margaret!" Lord Orrick exclaimed to his wife, apparently ignoring her own presence there and insulting his guest. "I swear he is nothing but a thick-skulled arse."

"My lord, Elizabeth knows not of what you speak. Mayhap Lord Gavin should join us so we may sort this out to everyone's benefit?" Lady Margaret did not wait on her husband's answer but went to the door and spoke quietly to the servant outside.

A few minutes passed in an uncomfortable silence as they waited for Lord Gavin to arrive. His loud knock startled her, and a tremor of nervousness passed through her at what would be their first encounter since... since...so many things had passed between them. Not sure of how he would treat her now, she lowered her head and waited. Lord Orrick did not allow for pleasantries, launching immediately into questions of his guest.

"Gavin, Elizabeth has accepted my offer of sponsorship to the Gilbertines' community. What say you to that?"

She was not certain why he should have anything to say on the matter, but 'twas obvious that Lord Orrick did. Elizabeth clasped her hands in front of her to keep them from shaking. Her nervousness increased as she waited, as they waited on Lord Gavin's reply.

"The convent, Elizabeth? You're to enter the

convent?" His voice was gruff and she imagined she could hear pain in it.

"Aye, my lord. Lord Orrick has been more than generous in his offer. 'Twould seem a good place for me." She did not look at him. She could not.

"I told you of my plan to make that offer, Gavin. You knew it was a possibility."

"Damn you for your meddling ways, Orrick," Gavin said, his voice more threatening for its softness. Elizabeth felt the tension in the room growing and knew that it involved more than simply her decision to leave.

"Do you have nothing to say to Elizabeth, Gavin? No offer to make to her?"

Lord Orrick moved to her side and faced Lord Gavin with the stance that men use when challenging each other. She could wait no longer and cause no more problems for either of these men who had championed her in some way or another for the past year.

Though she knew it was inappropriate, she stepped closer to Lord Gavin and placed her hand on his chest. She had not the courage to meet his gaze. "My lord, I am at peace with this decision. Do not feel that you must make some offer that you do not want to. Or that is not one makes to a wh—"

"Do not call yourself that!" he yelled, making her take a step back. "We both know you are not. There is much more to you than you admit, and I refuse to let you use that word again."

He reached out and took her shoulders in his hands,

pulling her closer. Lord Orrick and Lady Margaret did not look away from this wanton display, though Elizabeth was certain they had to be horrified.

"Lass," he said quietly, "look at me."

She slowly tilted her head. Instead of finding the anger in his voice, she found his eyes filled with softness and caring. 'Twould be her downfall now. "My lord?"

"I want you to return to my village with me. Once the weather breaks, I will take you back to my home and my clan."

"As your leman, my lord? To serve as your mistress until you marry again?" Those were her only options. Then what would she do when he married, for she could not stay and would have no place else to go. And she could not watch him marry another, knowing that her love for him would be for naught.

"Nay, Elizabeth. Be my wife."

She laughed out at his words, feeling her control slip away as the pain pierced her heart. Shaking, she could not breathe as she tried to understand why she was punished yet again. Just when she thought she'd found a way to cleanse her soul of the sins it bore and a way to be at peace, he tempted her with the one thing she craved yet could not have. At another time, in another life and place, marrying Gavin MacLeod would have fulfilled all of her dreams. Now the offer simply increased the punishment she would have to bear.

"Elizabeth," he said, squeezing her to bring her attention back to him. "Will you marry me?"

She pulled out of his grasp before she forced out the words that would damn her forever in his eyes. "I fear I cannot marry you, my lord, for I am already married."

"What?" he bellowed as he staggered back from her. "You are married?"

Lord Orrick took his ladywife by her hand and began to walk toward the door when Lord Gavin stopped them. "Oh no, my meddling friend. You put me on the quest to discover her truths, you will stay now and learn them with me."

So, her words to him about being a nobleman amusing himself with a lower woman were true. It had upset him at the time and now she knew why. But encouraging him to use her until he found out about her past was cruel. And not something she would have expected from Lord Orrick. Ah, 'twould seem that all noblemen can turn when their desires are thwarted as she had stymied his in his search for her past. This had all been about finding her weakness and using it to discover that which she would not disclose freely. And Lord Gavin had found it.

"I am married, my lord," she said, trying not to let the despair she felt enter her voice. "And have been since I was ten-and-six." She faced him now.

"Who was your husband?" Gavin asked. "Did he die and leave you unprotected? Have you no family to keep you from wh—?" He did not say the final word.

"My husband *is* a wealthy merchant in York who decided he no longer wanted me as wife. The deal he made with my father did not give him the heir he desperately wanted, so he got rid of me."

"Do you mean he put you aside, Elizabeth? What did the priest say? Or your father? Surely he fought against this?" Lady Margaret asked. The lady stepped to her side and Elizabeth felt some measure of comfort in having a woman nearby. Especially a noblewoman, who understood all of the machinations in a noble marriage.

"My father would not let him put me aside, for he believed it would cast aspersions on his good name. So, my husband did what he did best. He made a arrangements with some men to take me in the night and to be certain that I was found by my father with all of them. My father believed, as Kennard had hoped, that I had proved myself a whore and not worthy of his support or his name. A bastard daughter is good for so few things and if I was not worth gold in the match with the merchant, my father wanted nothing to do with me."

Lady Margaret's face drained of all its color and her husband noticed it, too. Lord Orrick took hold of her arm to support her as she stood. After a moment or two, Lady Margaret waved him off. "He did not secure you a place in a convent?"

"Nay, my lady. Kennard sold me to a brothel outside Carlisle and had found a new, fruitful wife when I last saw him. My father refused to see me once Kennard bought his silence in exchange for half my dowry returned to him."

"Half your dowry returned to your father?" the lady asked.

"Kennard would have kept it all since it was my disgrace that brought the marriage to an end, but to smooth things over and to keep my father from meddling, he offered him half of it back. 'Twas a sizable amount, enough to soothe any damages to his name or esteem done by his illegitimate whore of a daughter."

She could still hear the words spewing forth from Kennard and her father. Everything was her fault, for if she had conceived an heir for Kennard, none of this would have happened. If God had not granted her an heir, then 'twas surely a sign that she was sinful. Probably from her whore of a mother, who bore her out of the bonds of marriage, Kennard had said. Blood will tell, blood always tells....

Silence filled the room and she could look at no one, especially not Lord Gavin. Now he knew that she was married, put aside and truly a whore, sleeping with men other than her wedded husband. She could not bear to see the anger and disappointment in his eyes, for she knew he carried some noble idea in his mind that she was more than she truly was.

"So, my lord," she said, finally chancing a look at him, "I am not free to marry you, even if I wished it to be so."

Whatever reaction she expected, she did not receive it. She even thought he might wish her well in her new life of penance and service at the convent, now knowing the sins she must pay for. She thought he might argue with her over the vows she could not break. And part of her hoped he would ask her to go with him anyway, knowing that they each had feelings for the other.

Instead, he nodded at Lord Orrick and Lady Margaret and left the room without ever acknowledging her again. Elizabeth thought her heart had broken, in that moment, but it wasn't until she heard a few hours later that Lord Gavin had left Silloth, with no word on his return, that she knew the true pain of heartbreak.

NINE

The last day of the year arrived as gray and stormy as the month of days before it, but at least Elizabeth was in her own cottage. She could tolerate no more of the comments being made by the inhabitants of Silloth about her and Lord Gavin. The women took her side, for surely she was not the first woman to give herself in love to a man who then forsook her. The men did not understand how any harlot could have expected more than what she got—a fine tupping by a nobleman whom, they were sure, had left her some trinket to cover the cost of her services.

In spite of the celebrations going on around her, Elizabeth found it difficult not to give in to the desolation she felt inside. The feasting and mummery and joyous marking of Christ's birth and the end of the year all made it worse to be there and not be able to join in with the inhabitants of Lord Orrick's village.

The hostilities between the men and women who took sides over the situation of the Scot and the whore grew until the day after Christ's Mass when she finally sought permission to go to her cottage. Lord Orrick looked as though he might refuse at first, however once Lady Margaret spoke to him, he agreed to her request and even sent one of the stable-boys along with some supplies. Apparently, he and the lady wanted some measure of peace in their household as the year came to an end.

Now ensconced in her own place, with enough food and drink and peat to last for several weeks, Elizabeth decided to take the time to prepare herself for her new life. She understood now that in accepting Lord Gavin's invitation and enjoying those last few nights of bliss with him, she had tempted fate or offended the Almighty. And her punishment had been the awful exposure of her sinful past before the man she loved.

However, when she remembered hearing him speak of his love to her that night or when she woke in the night still feeling his touch on her skin, she was not completely penitent. Nay, she even longed for those nights and days when she had given herself to him. No matter the end they had come to, she would always treasure the memories of those nights with him.

The sun barely stayed up a few hours that day and Elizabeth allowed herself the luxury of a candle until she was finally ready to sleep. The winds howled outside and the ground was now covered with a layer of snow. No one would be going out this night. Somehow the end of the year made her maudlin and she took out her mother's ring and the silken scarf she'd managed to save from her life before.

Holding them, she cried out all of her grief for all she had lost. The tears flowed freely, something that she had never allowed to happen before, not even during her worst and lowest moments. Finally, at some time in the dark of the night she fell asleep.

The rapping on her door startled her awake. No fool would be out at this time in this weather. And she knew that Lord Orrick had announced that she would be leaving for the Gilbertines so that no man in his demesne would bother her. There was no one who needed her, so she feared opening the door. Then a voice called out to her.

"Mistress Elizabeth? Are you in there?"

The winds obscured the voice, but she thought it might be the miller's son. What could he want now? She unlatched the door but held on to the leather strap as tightly as she could as she let the door open an inch or two to see for certain. Aye. 'Twas Liam indeed. She let him in and pulled the door closed.

He was wet and stood before her without saying anything. Then he stuttered some words to her in what sounded like Gaelic and held out some wrapped packages to her. He stood silently as she opened them to find a loaf of bread, a jug of ale and a chunk of peat. Just as she was about to ask him the reason for his visit, the door flew open and he was dragged out from behind.

She went to the door, intent on following and finding out what had happened, when her path was blocked by a huge man wrapped in plaid. It took a moment for her to realize that Lord Gavin had returned and stood before her.

"He got the words all wrong, but what should I expect from a scrawny, young Sassenach like that. He was supposed to wish you good luck and prosperity in this new year, but I do not want to tell you what he really said."

Lord Gavin crossed the threshold into her cottage and she backed away to give him room. The cloaks he wore were covered in snow and he pushed them off, dropping them in a pile by the door.

"I would have been here sooner, lass, but I needed to find a dark-haired young man to lead the way in. I did not want to jeopardize your future by being the First Footer this night. Then I had to convince him to accompany me in the storm. It was not a pretty thing to watch."

Elizabeth could not believe her eyes. He stood before her and still she blinked again and again to see if he disappeared. He did not. He had been thoughtful enough to find the right man to step in her door this first night. She could feel tears gathering as she watched him smile and as the heart she thought was broken began to pound in her chest.

"Ah, lass, I have so much to apologize for. Will you hear me out before throwing me back out in the storm?"

"You are welcome, my lord." His expression darkened and he frowned at her. "You are welcome, Gavin."

"May I sit?" he asked, pointing at the small bench. Her cottage did not have the fine furniture he was accustomed to.

"Please. Can I get you something to drink? Or eat? I brought some of Lady Margaret's wassail from the keep if you'd like." She pointed to the small jug near the hearth. Then, Elizabeth reached for the bread Liam had given her. Gavin's hand on hers stopped her.

"First, lass, I have been waiting for weeks to do this."

He pulled her close and kissed the breath right out of her. She was weak—she did not resist the embrace or the heated kisses he touched on her mouth. Indeed, she opened to him and breathed him in as he tasted her over and over again. Then, in too short a time, he released her and stepped back.

"If we keep up with that, I will never tell you what I came to tell you." He began pacing the extent of the cottage. He could only take a few steps before turning back the other way. Finally he looked at her, took a deep breath and let it out, and began the story he hoped would convince her to be with him.

"You gave me quite a surprise that morning, Elizabeth. Of all the answers I could have imagined, you being married was not one of them. Then when I heard your words, I wanted to kill someone." His hands fisted as he remembered the terrible things, she had begun to believe about herself. "True men do not blame women for their shortcomings or failures. True men accept their responsibilities."

"But my—" "But, Gavin, I was the one who failed. I was the one who did not give my husband an heir. I was the one…"

"Who did all that she could and still carries the guilt on her shoulders for the ruthless, worthless men who will not accept their part in her downfall." She believed all the wrong things they'd told her. All the filthy names they called her. She did not believe she was worthy of forgiveness, and she had done nothing that needed forgiving. "I went to York to find the slime who you called husband. I needed to find out the truth."

"You went to York? You saw Kennard?" Her voice shook as did her hands. "What did he say?"

"I did not speak to him. I spoke to your father and mother."

"My mother? You spoke to her? How does she fare?" Tears streamed down her face now and his heart was torn by the sadness he saw in her eyes.

The poor lass. She had gone to her father when she'd managed to escape from the whorehouse in Hayton and he threatened to turn out her mother if she tried to seek his help again. Knowing it was her life or her mother's, Elizabeth had walked away and asked for nothing. And the bastard had granted her nothing. His hands tightened again as he remembered wanting to strangle the life from his worthless body at his plain admission of abandonment.

"She is well and being taken care of as your father promised. He is good for that."

110

"What did he say?"

"I wish I could tell you otherwise, but he is unrepentant for his treatment of you or his desire for what Kennard offered him to betray you."

"And Kennard?"

She looked as though she would pass out, so he gathered her close and sat down with her on the pallet. "Take a few deep breaths, lass." When she had followed his directions and some color had returned to her cheeks, he continued with his story.

"Kennard is dead."

"Dead? Dead? Did you… ?"

Perhaps it was his satisfied smile that made her suspect he played a part in the man's demise. He could not help but be happy that the one who had set out to destroy the woman he loved was dead and rotting in his grave.

"I confess I would have if I had found him alive after seeing the damage done to you for naught but his own greed. But he died of consumption sometime after you arrived here in Silloth. And the brother whom he hated more than he hated you has inherited all that Kennard tried to keep to himself."

Elizabeth leaned back against him in shock from the news, but he savored the feel of her anyway in his arms after these weeks without her. Pure rage had forced his feet out of that room after she spoke of her past. Fury had driven him through storms and over hills and mountains to seek the truth that even she did not know. Anger alone sustained him and gave him the strength to search for the truth so that he could give her something of value.

No one, not even the lowest creature on God's earth, deserved the treatment she described that day and he knew that he must seek out her past. And give her some hope for a future. Even if she did not accept him, he felt content knowing that she had given him a reason for living. Even if for a short time, he was needed again.

"My offer still stands, Elizabeth, although I am sure that you will examine the choices you have now that you are a widow of means."

She sat up and faced him. "What do you mean?"

"Apparently, your marriage agreement provided that half of your dowry would be returned to you if Kennard should die before you. Kennard purposely kept his other deal with your father secret and never changed his will or the marriage settlement papers. So, the other half of your dowry was returned to your father. I confess I had to do some persuading, but I have a bag of gold in my cloak that belongs to you now. There is enough in there for you to go wherever you would like and live well when you get there."

Her mouth dropped open and he reached up and gently closed it. He could only imagine what she was thinking. The questions she must have. The choices she could make now.

"Why? Why did you do this?" She pushed the hair from her face and rubbed her eyes. "You did not know me until just a short time ago. Why would you involve yourself in the cause of a stranger?"

He smiled, knowing he had asked himself the same thing over and over as he traveled across the length and breadth of England searching for her truths. And he knew both of his reasons.

"Part of the reason is nothing more than arrogant selfishness. After months and months of feeling unneeded by anyone, you needed me. You did not know that I would pursue this for you, but you needed to know the truth and I could find it out for you. I was finally needed and it satisfied something within me."

"You foolish man! You are needed. Messages have arrived almost daily asking about your return to your village. Asking for your guidance on matters big and small. Lord Orrick has felt quite put-upon trying to cover for your absence." She touched his cheek and kissed him lightly. "You are needed."

She leaned back into his arms and they stayed just so for several minutes. Was he foolish? Was his arrogant pride standing in the way of accepting his true place in his family? Was there something that an old warrior could offer the new generation of the clan?

"And the other reason you became my champion?" she whispered from within his embrace.

"That should be obvious to anyone who has the Gaelic. As I told you that first night you gave yourself to me—I love you, lass, with all my heart." He laughed now. "And I think you understood my words?"

"My grandmam would say something like that, so I

thought I did. But I dared not believe it could be true. A warrior and a whore?"

"A man and a woman," he insisted. "Elizabeth, I know you have the chance to start a new life wherever you'd like, with none of the past following you. I know that I am much older and you probably want a younger man, someone closer to your age. But I would ask you again to be my wife and come home with me to the Highlands."

She climbed to her feet and walked a few paces from him, deep in thought. 'Twas true—she could leave here and begin a new life where no one knew of the things she'd suffered in the past. With the gold in his cloak, she could afford a house of her own, servants, and more. She did not need him now that he had given her the truth. He waited, barely able to breathe, for her decision.

"I cannot give you children," she announced to him. "I am barren."

"I have bairns already, love," he replied. "And they have bairns. I need no more." He meant it. His need for heirs had been fulfilled in his first marriage. He was free to marry for love this time if she would have him.

"I had thought never to marry again, Gavin. Now, I do not have to and yet I find myself wanting to accept your offer."

"Then accept it, love, and be my wife."

As had happened the first time she came to his chamber to help with his bath, a myriad of emotions passed over her face. He stood watching, knowing that he could do nothing to interfere or it would be as worthless as her first marriage had been. Then a smile filled her face and she gave him the words he needed and wanted and longed to hear.

"Husband and wife?" she asked.

"If you wish it."

"And my past? Can you forget what I have done?" Her voice shook again as she asked this. He knew this was now the only thing holding her back from moving forward.

"So long as you do not hold mine against me, lass. I am not the saint you believe me to be."

"I suspected as much. But since I love you so much, I will try to overlook that."

"You love me?"

"Aye, Gavin, I love you and want to be your wife."

And, with her first step toward him on the first night of the year of our Lord 1200, Elizabeth gave him everything he wanted.

EPILOGUE

"You are going to be insufferable now, are you not, my lord?" Margaret whispered to her husband as they sat at table.

The last days of the holiday celebrations continued on around them and everyone took part in the feasting. Pipers and other musicians made merry tunes that brought some to their feet in a dance. Orrick's yule log, now much smaller, burned brightly in the large hearth of the hall, offering its heat and aroma to one and all there. This time of year was special to her husband, and her heart was gladdened to see that her preparations and arrangements had once more proved pleasing to him.

"But my love, you were the one who first gave me the thought that they would suit well together," he whispered back. "And 'twould seem that you were correct again."

Orrick lifted her hand and kissed it. He even turned her hand palm up and touched the sensitive skin of her wrist with his tongue, knowing full well what it would do to her. And she knew that the shivers that ran through her were obvious to him.

"Two more of your wounded creatures will leave you now. Will you search for more?"

He never looked for them, they always discovered him and the sanctuary he offered. And as she learned many years before, when she found him, he never asked anyone to leave.

"I am certain that others will come, my love. Just as long as you are at my side."

He gifted her with the smoldering look that even now, after twenty years together, still set her heart to racing and made her palms sweat and her mouth water. The look that promised so much. The look that foretold of pleasures in the long nights of winter and love in the days.

"I will always be yours, my lord." 'Twas the truth. Nothing would part them. "*Waes hael,* my lord." She lifted a cup to him.

He lifted his to her and replied, "*Drinc hael,* my lady."

They sipped from their cups and she watched as Orrick surveyed the hall and his people, the smile on his face telling of his satisfaction with all he saw. His words but confirmed what she already knew.

"All is well in Silloth. All is well."

Please turn the page to enjoy an excerpt from

The King's Mistress

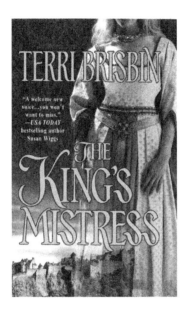

Here's the scene from THE KING'S MISTRESS when Orrick of Silloth and Marguerite of Alencon meet for the first time when King Henry II orders them to marry. And let's say, it doesn't go well!

"My lady," he said as he acknowledged her obeisance and held out his hand. "Please rise now."

The softness of her fingers against his work-roughened hand sent fire through him. And when she finally raised her gaze to his, he knew he was lost.

Her hair did indeed reach nigh to the floor in spite of some decorations and jewels that were woven into the curls surrounding her face. His hands itched to touch it, feel it, even bring it to his face and inhale the fragrance of her that was carried by it. When she moved her head, her hair cascaded in flowing waves over her shoulders and arms and down her back. In an instant, his mind pictured her how she would be later in the night—in his bed, naked, with only her hair to shield her.

Shocked by his carnal reaction to simply meeting her, Orrick knew he must tame this beast within him or appear the barbarian she surely thought him to be. Stepping back and motioning to a bench, he allowed her to sit. A few steps across the chamber and he felt a bit more in control. Until she spoke.

"My lord Orrick, I am pleased to have this chance to meet you privately. My thanks for granting what must seem a strange request by a bride on her wedding day."

Soft and incredibly feminine, her voice carried within a hint of huskiness and once more his body betrayed him. That underlying tone would be evident as she cried out her pleasure in his bed. He saw her naked and writhing against him as he filled her with his seed and as their satisfaction poured forth from both of them in loud cries. He closed his eyes for a moment and then realized her power.

Orrick had come to this day aware of the gossip and the tales told about her ongoing liaisons with the king. He had armed himself with a healthy measure of suspicion so that he did not become anyone's fool in this. Believing that he did not make decisions with his cock, he had felt completely at ease with his ability to assess the lady and the situation and handle all of it.

Fool!

In but a few moments, her beauty, her blatant sexuality and her silent promises about what would be his ensorcelled him. With a curtsy and a nod, with a shake of her hair and an enticing scent and with simple words she had ensnared him in her trap. Now he stood before her, hard as stone and wanting her more than he had ever wanted a woman. The urge, the need, to touch and taste and hold and have and fill and claim and mark her as his own grew until he feared it might overwhelm him. Looking around the chamber, he spied a small table with a jug and some goblets. He used it to break her spell.

"Wine, my lady?" He poured some for himself, managing not to spill it in spite of the way his hand shook. Without waiting for her reply, he filled a goblet for her and brought it to her.

"My thanks, Lord Orrick," she whispered as she lifted the wine to her mouth.

He watched as she finished her sip and as a drop of the sweet dark liquid began to trickle down from the corner of her lips. Even as his body moved forward to her, Marguerite used the tip of her tongue to catch it. He could not allow this to continue. Pulling his control around him, Orrick stepped back.

"And the reason for this meeting?"

"Why, to meet you, my lord! I know 'tis not so unusual for those of our status to marry without ever setting eyes on each other." She paused and let her gaze move over him in a provocative way. Just as he could almost feel her touch, she continued. "But His Grace, the king, allowed this breach of etiquette because we have long been friends."

"So I have heard, my lady."

There! He needed to let her know that he was no man's fool, not even the king's. He might be forced to take Henry's cast-off lover as wife, but Orrick would not pretend he did not know the real relationship between Henry and Marguerite. Not even to her, not even to assuage his own pride.

Her reaction surprised him. She stood and handed him the cup. Walking to the door, she faced him. The soft expression on her face changed to a much harder one, one that sapped most of the beauty from her features. She stood taller and stared at him with a look that sent icy chills down his spine.

He had seen the sensual, enticing, womanly Marguerite at first.

This was the angry, controlling, warriorlike Marguerite.

"Although I owe you nothing, Orrick of Silloth, I know that you are forced to this marriage as I am and want you to know the truth."

He lifted the cup to his mouth and swallowed the wine in one mouthful. "And which truth would that be, my lady?" Did she plan to admit that she had shared the king's bed and mayhap even had his love?

"This marriage will not happen. I am somewhat sorry that you have been drawn into this misunderstanding between the king and me, so I wish to warn you of what is to come."

Was there some other plotting going on? Did the king have some punishment in mind for some imagined wrongdoing on his or his father's part? Why this sham of marriage if Henry planned to arrest him on some charge? His gut tightened and he worried about what would happen to his people if he were imprisoned or hanged. Finally, he took a breath and asked.

"And what is to come?"

"My lord Henry is simply using this charade to put me in my place. I overstepped myself and he wishes me to know what he could do if he is displeased with me. I fear you have been caught up in a lovers' quarrel."

The roiling in his stomach lessened a bit as his own

suspicions grew. Would Henry go through all of this very public display of giving her in marriage and then default at the last moment? Orrick had signed most of the papers involving the transfer of property and titles and, indeed, had received a portion of the gold promised already. Aye, a king could undo all of that with a word, but would he?

"Henry will call off the wedding today?" he asked, searching for something more. His instincts told him there was much more going on here.

"Of course he will! He loves me and will not give me away to some northern lord who never attends court." She must have seen his look of disbelief for she added, "I was raised as consort for a king, not some…some…"

"Barbarian of mixed blood, my lady?"

Oh, her words had been duly reported to him just after she'd uttered them. He had chosen to ignore them for in the strange situation it was sometimes difficult to discern who said what to whom about whom. The challenge had been offered and accepted—there would be no more of the courtly niceties between them in this conversation. She did not soften her stance at all; indeed she seemed to be strengthened by the fact that he knew how she felt about him.

"Just so, my lord. Surely the king will find a more suitable match for you from among his English nobles. I fear I am far too accustomed to living at court and in my own country that it would make me too sad to move so far from it."

And too far from Henry. Those words remained

unspoken, but they echoed in his head as though she had shouted them.

"Is your purpose in telling me this to force me to Henry with a request to call off this arrangement? Is that what you hope for?"

She looked away as though she was not going to answer and then turned back and met his stare. "I was simply trying to save you the humiliation of facing the court at a wedding without a bride at your side. I thought you should know that Henry will claim me and not allow you to marry me as you've been asked to do."

Her voice was soft and he could almost believe that she was sincere. For a brief moment he did believe her, and then a stab of pity tore at his heart as he realized the truth of the matter.

She believed it.

Marguerite believed that Henry would step in and stop the wedding. She was either ignorant of the arrangements already in place, or she was simply denying it to herself. He guessed that, after years of being the king's favorite, 'twas too difficult to admit that she no longer held his affections or that unofficial place of honor within the court. The gossips had not named a new paramour to the king, but it would simply be a matter of time before one was identified and took her place.

How could it feel to have lived less than a score of years and already be considered a castoff? Loved, abandoned and now given away to a stranger. From the look in her eyes and the tilt of her chin, she did not want pity from him or anyone else. So, he would give her none. But as she had warned him, he would offer one of his own.

"I, too, believe that humiliation will be the order of the day, Marguerite, but fear you will feel its bite and not I. I suggest you prepare yourself and protect your heart if you wish to survive it."

She blinked rapidly as though trying to understand, and he knew it was time to leave. He put his hand to the knob of the door and she stepped aside, allowing him to pass without comment.

There was nothing else to say to her. They were both pawns, playing out the moves of the game in front of the Plantagenet court and before the game master himself.

God help them all.

Meet Terri Brisbin

RWA RITA®-nominated, award-winning and *USA Today* best-selling author **Terri Brisbin** is a mom, a wife, grandmom(!) and a dental hygienist who has sold more than 3 million copies of her historical and paranormal romance novels and novellas in more than 25 countries and 20 languages. Her current and upcoming historical and paranormal/fantasy romances are published by Harlequin Historicals, Penguin Random House, St. Martin's Press/Swerve and independently, too.

Connect with her on
Facebook @TerriBrisbinAuthor
Twitter @Terri_Brisbin
Instagram @TerriBrisbin

If you'd liked to keep up with Terri's news, events, special goodies and giveaways and upcoming and ongoing releases, please sign up for her newsletter on her website – Terri promises not to clog your emailbox!

TerriBrisbin.com

Printed in Great Britain
by Amazon

50705850R00079